MONSTERSTREET

THE HALLOWEENERS

2

MONSTERSTREET

THE HALLOWEENERS

J. H. REYNOLDS

KATHERINE TEGEN BOOKS
An Imprint of HarperCollins Publishers

Katherine Tegen Books is an imprint of
HarperCollins Publishers.

Monsterstreet #2: The Halloweeners
For information address HarperCollins Children's
Books, a division of HarperCollins Publishers,
195 Broadway, New York, NY 10007.
www.harpercollinschildrens.com

Library of Congress Control Number: 2018968549
ISBN 978-0-06-286938-8 (trade bdg.)
ISBN 978-0-06-286937-1 (pbk.)

Typography by Ray Shappell
19 20 21 22 23   PC/BRR   10 9 8 7 6 5 4 3 2 1

First Edition
Also available in a hardcover edition.

This book is dedicated to the memory of Clay Rodman, my best friend in the neighborhood where I grew up, with whom I shared a magical Halloween night long ago.

1

THE HOUSE AT THE
END OF MAPLE STREET

Fisher gripped the straps of his backpack as he trudged down Maple Street, gazing in each window at the silhouettes of boys and girls putting on homemade costumes and nibbling on fresh-baked treats. Jack-o'-lanterns grinned at him from cobwebbed porches. Blow-up monsters and plastic gravestones loomed on leaf-covered lawns. And the sugary scent of candy wafted through the crisp autumn air, enchanting his nostrils. It seemed every house on the block was decorated for Halloween.

All except one.

The house at the end of Maple Street looked just as ordinary as it did on any other day of the year. There wasn't a single pumpkin, not one fake spider, not even a sign that greeted guests with *Happy Halloween!*

Fisher walked up to the door of the house, turned the brass knob, and stepped inside. He reached down to pet his cat, and heard his mom's voice echoing from the kitchen. . . .

". . . Yes, I accept the position. We'll be there before Thanksgiving. I'm very much looking forward to this opportunity."

Fisher peeked around the corner just as his mom hung up the phone. She was wearing jeans and a sweater, and her short brown hair looked darker in the shadows where she sat.

"Who was that?" Fisher asked.

His mom winced, startled. "No one."

"It had to be someone," Fisher pried.

His mom sighed.

"If you must know, I was offered a vice principal position in that town on the coast I was telling you about."

"We're moving . . . again?" Fisher's voice reeked of disappointment.

"You know how much I don't like being here," his mom said. "I lived in this town, and in this house, long enough while I was growing up. I told you when we moved this summer that it was only a temporary stop for you and me after the divorce—until we could get settled somewhere better."

"But I'm just starting to get used to this place," Fisher said. "Some guys at school even asked me to go trick-or-treating with them tonight. Do you know how hard it is to get invited to something at a new school? Everyone's had the same friends since kindergarten."

"You can make new friends after we move," his mom replied.

"That's what you said last time, and so that's what I'm trying to do," Fisher pointed out.

"There's no negotiating on this," his mom said.

Fisher felt the hot fire of anger burning in his chest, and he tried to push it down deep where he kept all his feelings. But it was too much to hold in.

"If you and Dad hadn't gotten a divorce, I never would have had to leave my friends in the first place!" he erupted like a volcano.

His mom was silent. Fisher knew mentioning the divorce was a powerful weapon, and he only used it when he felt he had no other choice.

"You're entitled to your own feelings about it. And so am I," his mom said, but her words felt cold. Like she wasn't listening to him. Ever since the divorce, he felt like he and his mom were living on two different planets with nothing in common but their last name.

"Why do you have to be so selfish?" Fisher mumbled.

"What did you say?"

Fisher debated whether to say it again. Instead, he said something worse.

"Dad wouldn't make me move again."

He saw the color of anger fill his mom's face.

"Well, your dad isn't here, is he? And as long

as you're living under my roof, you'll live by my rules."

"I hate your rules!" Fisher shouted, still unable to control his temper.

"That's it, young man. You're grounded," she said in her principal-like voice.

"But what about Halloween?"

"Doesn't make any difference to me what day it is," she returned. "You know I don't care for Halloween anyway."

"But Mom!"

"With that attitude, you can stay in your room for the entire weekend. I've already put some moving boxes upstairs, so you can get an early start on packing."

"That's not fair!"

"Okay. The next month! Keep it up and you'll be grounded for the rest of sixth grade."

He stared at her for a long moment, then decided arguing would only make things worse. He turned and walked up the stairs to his bedroom and lay down in his reading tent, where he kept his stash of comic books and monster figurines.

He heard his mom shout from downstairs, "By the way, I have to chaperone the Halloween dance at the high school later, so I'll bring your dinner up before I leave. And no TV while I'm gone—I don't want you having nightmares from all those monster movies that will be on tonight!"

Fisher glanced across the room to the pile of cardboard boxes waiting to be filled. He had just unpacked everything a few months before, and now his mom was making him do it all again.

Why can't Mom just listen to me for once? And why can't she just let me go trick-or-treating?

Right then, a staticky sound buzzed over the walkie-talkie in his backpack.

A boy's raspy voice came through. "The meeting's about to start. You coming or what?"

2

SECRET HIDEOUT

Fisher ripped the white sheet from his bed and used his pocketknife to cut out two oval holes for his eyes.

"This will have to do for my costume," he whispered, tucking the ghost sheet into his backpack and climbing out the window.

As soon as his feet hit the ground, he ran to his bike. Then he pedaled as fast as he could into the forest at the edge of the neighborhood, just as the boy on the walkie-talkie had told him to do.

The afternoon sun beamed through the skeleton trees, bathing the woods with an eerie autumn glow. Red and brown leaves crunched beneath his tires as he passed an old graveyard, running his fingers over the spikes of the rusted iron fence. A hundred yards up, he arrived at a giant oak tree three times the size of any others in sight. Its limbs were gnarled, twisted, and full of knots. A deep hollow stared out from its trunk like the eye socket of a skull.

Fisher saw three other bikes lying on the ground near the base of the tree, and he knew he was in the right place.

High above, a tree house was cradled within its limbs, hidden in camouflage.

A handmade wooden sign hung on its side:

THE HALLOWEENERS
Est. 1955

"Hey, I'm here!" he shouted, a bit nervous.

A moment later, a boy wearing a tuxedo with a red bow tie and a black top hat looked over the edge of the tree house.

But . . .

The boy was missing his head.

A mysterious empty space existed between the neck of his suit and his floating top hat. Fisher soon noticed a wire connecting the two, creating the illusion of an invisible man.

"Champ?" Fisher called up, recognizing the boy's voice.

Two hands peeled open the chest of the tuxedo, and a plump face dotted with freckles peeked out.

"Took you long enough!" Champ teased, shoving a handful of potato chips into his mouth. "Just pull the rope in the hollow and come on up!"

Fisher reached into the tree hollow and pulled on a rope hidden in the shadows. A secret ladder was triggered, clattering down to him from above.

He climbed, rung by rung, and opened the secret door at the bottom of the hideout.

Champ stood above him, waiting.

"Can you guess what I am?" Champ asked.

"An invisible magician?" Fisher guessed.

"Soooo close. But no," Champ said, smiling his goofy smile. "I'm an invisible candy-snatcher!"

He grabbed a pillowcase from the nearby bookshelf and acted like he was stealing candy out of thin air and adding it to his plunder.

"Cool illusion," Fisher affirmed. "Did you make it yourself?"

"Yeah," Champ said. "I asked my dad for help, but he was too busy, so I just did it myself like I do every year. Anyway, come meet the guys."

Fisher felt a knot of nervousness in his stomach as they approached the other boys. He looked around at the magnificent tree house. Plastered against the walls were movie posters and books, monster figurines and handmade models. The entire place was a museum of strange, macabre relics.

"Guys, this is Fisher. He's the one I was telling you about who sits beside me in social studies," Champ said.

No one in the tree house seemed to care Fisher was there. He sensed he wasn't the first person who Champ had invited to their secret hideout. And he hoped they would like him enough to let him stick around.

"That there is Squirrel," Champ said, pointing to a tall, skinny boy dressed like a vampire, sitting in the corner at a milk crate table. He was holding a ruler and geometry compass, drawing something onto a large sheet of paper.

Squirrel nodded to Fisher, barely looking up.

Champ continued, "He's super smart. All GT classes. He likes to be in control, so he's our secretary and treasurer."

"What are you?" Fisher asked Champ.

Champ held up his bag of potato chips and winked. "Food service."

Fisher smiled and observed Squirrel, who was diligently working on his project.

"If you can't tell, he's supposed to be a vampire," Champ added.

"*Vegetarian* vampire," Squirrel corrected him, breaking out of his trance. "This year, our costumes are supposed to be ironic interpretations of our fears."

"Whatever," Champ said, then continued, "Behind the bookshelf is Pez. He's our president. Mainly because he could beat us up if we ever tried to take his place."

Fisher glanced around the side of the bookshelf and saw a boy dressed as a swamp monster lying on a couch and tossing a baseball up in the air and catching it in his mitt.

"I'm a dehydrated swamp creature," Pez said, then sucked water through a straw connected to an Ozark container rigged with shoulder straps.

Champ whispered to Fisher. "Pez was bit by a moccasin in the creek last summer and nearly died, so now he's afraid of water. Even though his dad's the head swim coach at the high school."

Pez stood from the couch and walked toward Fisher.

"What Champ isn't telling you is that I have more home runs, touchdowns, and three-pointers than any kid at school. I just don't like to swim anymore, that's all," Pez explained. "Anyway, what are you supposed to be, new kid?"

Fisher held up his white bedsheet, timidly.

"A ghost sheet?" Pez mumbled, unimpressed, then walked away.

"As long as it's an ironic interpretation of a fear, it will work," Squirrel called from his workshop space.

"You could be . . . a 'ghost who's afraid of ghosts,'" Champ suggested.

"Hey, that's good," Fisher said, pulling the sheet over his head. He peered out the eyeholes and playfully made a moaning sound like a ghost. "I mean, everyone's afraid to die. Right?"

"Champ told us you drew some pretty rad jack-o'-lanterns in class," Pez continued. "Says you seem to know a lot about monsters. Is it true?"

"I know some stuff. I have the entire collection of *Monster Magazine* and have seen just about every scary movie ever made."

"That's somewhat impressive," Pez said. "But the real question is . . . do you think you have what it takes to be a Halloweener?"

Pez stared down at Fisher, dissecting him with his eyes. Fisher gulped, feeling warmth rush into his head and sweat form in his palms.

Fisher removed his ghost sheet, then asked the question he somehow knew he'd dread asking. . . .

"What's a Halloweener?"

3

THE HALLOWEENERS

They stared at Fisher like they couldn't believe he had asked the question. Either that, or that the answer was so secret that they would have to kill him if they told him.

Pez picked up a wooden gavel and knocked on the tree-stump table at the center of the tree house three times.

Squirrel, Champ, and Fisher joined him.

"The Halloweeners," Pez began, "is the greatest, most secret club that's ever existed in the history of the world. A Halloweener is someone who's sworn to preserve and protect Halloween at all costs."

"Yeah, and to get in, you have to profess Halloween as your favorite holiday. And devote yourself to learning everything about it," Squirrel added. "Most important, you have to take the oath to uphold the Three Sacred Laws of Halloween."

"Three Sacred Laws?" Fisher asked.

Squirrel stepped forward, looking like a professor.

"One . . . no smashing jack-o'-lanterns," he said. "They're the most sacred symbol of Halloween."

"Two . . . no stealing candy," Champ added, then mumbled out the side of his mouth, "It's my least favorite law."

"Three . . . no disrespecting the Dead," Pez warned. "Halloween is the one night of the year when the Dead wander among the Living. That's why our tree house is next to the graveyard. We're their protectors."

Fisher glanced out the tree-house window to the iron gates of the cemetery below. They looked like a doorway into another world. Giant oak trees canopied the hundreds of gravestones rising up from the ground like cracked teeth. Fisher imagined all the corpses lying beneath the ground, rotting away in their dark, suffocating boxes.

He gulped.

"What happens if someone breaks one of the rules?" he asked.

Pez, Squirrel, and Champ stared at him as if he had just committed blasphemy.

"Bad things will happen," Squirrel warned him. "And you'll be excommunicated from the ancient order of the Halloweeners forever."

Fisher put up his hands in surrender.

"Got it. No breaking the rules," he confirmed.

"So . . . ," Pez continued in his most serious voice. "Do you think you have what it takes to join the club?"

Fisher thought of all the cafeteria lunches when he had sat alone at a table while everyone else sat with their friends. These were the first guys who wanted to be his friends since he had moved. Plus, they loved Halloween as much as he did.

"I'm in," Fisher professed. "I want to be a Halloweener."

Pez smiled. "Good. Then you have to help us win the Halloween Games. The three categories are costume contest, trick-or-treating competition, and jack-o'-lantern carving. And this year, we have a secret weapon."

"Secret weapon?" Champ asked excitedly.

Squirrel took the scroll from the milk crate where he had been diligently working and rolled it out over the tree-stump table. It was a map marked up with pencils, crayons, and colored markers. Fisher had never seen such a meticulously detailed blueprint.

The top of it read:

The Halloweeners' Trick-or-Treat Map

"My parents are in charge of the festival every year," Squirrel explained. "They judge by candy weight, not quantity. So we want to get as much poundage as we can before we weigh in. I've marked all the houses with candy baskets in red. But remember, the Second Law of Halloween is no stealing candy, so we can only take as many pieces as the instructions on each basket allow. Got it?"

Fisher nodded, impressed that Squirrel had broken trick-or-treating down to a science.

"The blue houses here are the ones that give the biggest candy bars. We'll get those next," Squirrel said.

"This map is brilliant," Champ gushed. "Even better than the one you made last year."

"I like to improve on my designs," Squirrel said. "My dad says it's what successful people do."

Pez put his hand on Fisher's shoulder. "You help us win the Games and you'll be an official Halloweener by the end of the night. You still in?"

Fisher nodded.

"All right, then. What are we waiting for?" Pez asked.

He put his hand out over the Halloweener emblem carved into the center of the tree stump. It was a jack-o'-lantern filled with candy and resting against a gravestone—symbolizing the Three Laws of Halloween.

No smashing jack-o'-lanterns. No stealing candy. And no disrespecting the Dead.

Champ and Squirrel put their hands on top of Pez's hand.

Fisher respectfully stood aside and watched as the three of them chanted their ancient motto aloud: "Once a Halloweener, always a Halloweener. Till death and beyond!"

He envied their camaraderie, and wanted more than anything to join them.

It'd be nice to have friends like that, Fisher thought.

After they finished saying the motto, Pez put on his creature mask and strapped the water container to his back. Squirrel rolled up the scroll map and put it in his backpack. Champ buttoned his tuxedo and hid himself while Fisher covered himself with the ghost sheet again.

Together, the four boys scampered down the tree-house ladder and onto their bikes. They pedaled past the iron gates of the graveyard, through the woods, over the creek, across Old Joe's Pumpkin Farm, and back into the neighborhood of white picket fences, where swarms of costumed children reveled in the greatest night of the year.

The one night they could become anything they dreamed.

The night that would soon turn into a nightmare.

4

TRICK AND TREAT

The black paved streets looked like snakes slithering through the neighborhood. Jedi Knights and Avengers, scary clowns and one-eyed pirates all roamed from one door to the next, filling their buckets and pillowcases with a kaleidoscope of treats.

By the time the clock tower struck eight, the Halloweeners had each filled up two pillow-cases with candy.

Fisher stopped his bike and looked at an advertisement stapled to a telephone pole:

ALL-NIGHT MONSTER MARATHON AT THE DRIVE-IN!
SPONSORED BY BUGFRY CANDY FACTORY!
EVERYONE'S INVITED!

"We should tell our parents we're staying at each other's houses, and then sneak out and go to the monster marathon," Champ suggested.

"I'm game," Pez said. "You in, Fish?"

"I sort of already snuck out tonight, so yeah," Fisher agreed.

"Snuck out? On Halloween?" Champ asked.

"It's a long story—but the simple version is that I got grounded for talking back to my mom," Fisher explained.

"Bummer," Champ said. "Glad you broke out of mom jail."

They looked to Squirrel, but he was focused on more urgent matters.

"According to the map, we only have a few more houses left on this street," Squirrel said, pushing his plastic fangs back into place.

"We're going to win. I can feel it," Pez declared, peering out the eye slits of his mask.

"I still can't see anything," Champ said from inside his invisibility suit. "Pez, can you guide me with your hand again?"

Pez took a swig of water from his straw and reluctantly placed his reptilian hand on Champ's shoulder.

When they turned the corner, they saw something that shattered all their hopes of winning the Halloween Games. . . .

Across the street, four masked trick-or-treaters approached Mrs. Sanderson's front door. They were each wearing a black cloak and a skeleton mask. As soon as Mrs. Sanderson dropped candy into their buckets, they ran to the side of her house and switched out their disguises to pumpkin-head masks, then they went back to the old woman's door and rang the doorbell again.

"Trick or treat!" the Pumpkinheads cried,

and the old woman gave them more candy, not recognizing them from a few moments before.

"Sweet junipers," Squirrel proclaimed in awe, as if he was observing the holy grail of trick-or-treating strategies. "So that's how the Pumpkinheads win every year."

"You're supposed to be the one with all the ideas, Squirrel," Pez reminded him. "Why didn't you think of that?"

Squirrel shrugged in defeat.

They watched as the clever team of trick-or-treaters took off their masks and crossed the street toward them. As soon as they stepped out of the shadows, Fisher saw their faces.

"Well, if it isn't the Hallo*weenies*," the tallest girl taunted. She was wearing a witch's hat and carrying a broom. Her masks were tucked into the pockets of her cloak. "Is that all the candy you guys have gotten?"

Champ, Squirrel, Pez, and Fisher looked down at their pillowcases and realized how measly their plunder was compared to the girls'.

"Uh, we have more candy bags hidden in some bushes back there," Champ said, pointing aimlessly behind him.

"Riiight," the girl replied.

"We saw that trick you pulled on Mrs. Sanderson, Ava," Squirrel said accusingly. "That's against the rules."

"It's called trick-*and*-treating, dweebo," Ava replied. "We trick in order to get more treats." She paused and glanced at Fisher. "Who's the ghost kid?"

"This is Fisher," Champ said. "He's one of us now—well, almost."

"He might as well tattoo a giant 'L' on his forehead," Ava jabbed, and the girls around her all giggled. She then stepped closer to Fisher to try to glimpse his eyes through the cut-out holes. "Does he talk?"

"Yes, I talk," Fisher said, already not liking the girl one bit. He pointed to her pocket full of masks. "What are you supposed to be, anyway? A witch having an identity crisis?"

Champ laughed, but quickly stopped when Ava glared over at him.

"I'm an aviophobic witch, thank you very much."

"Avio—what?" Champ asked.

"Aviophobic. It means I'm afraid to fly," she explained. "I don't do airplanes, helicopters, or spaceships. My father's a pilot, so me being an aviophobe is extra ironic."

The boys stared at her blankly.

"Get it? A witch who's afraid to fly?" she explained, holding up her broom. "You guys should really try reading the dictionary sometime. And good luck finding all that stashed candy you hid! Maybe it's being protected by leprechauns and unicorns."

Ava and her posse of witches walked past the Halloweeners and toward the next house, swinging their pumpkin buckets full of candy. Fisher watched as she whispered some secret scheme to her minions. The other girls nodded at her command, then scattered like mice to carry out her surely sinister plot.

Fisher, Squirrel, Champ, and Pez stood on the corner of Burgundy and Sandalwood, looking lost and hopeless.

"Who was that?" Fisher asked.

"Ava Highwater," Pez said. "Our least favorite girl at school."

"I can't stand her," Squirrel said.

"Me neither," Champ added.

"Is she always like that?" Fisher asked.

"Let me put it this way—that was the nice version of her," Pez said.

"There's no way we can win now," Champ grumbled, staring into his half-empty pillowcase.

"We definitely won't win if we don't try," Fisher said.

"You're right," Pez agreed. "Bring out the map again, Squirrel. Let's hit up as many big-bar houses as we can with the hour we have left. All the baskets will be emptied by now, so the big bars are our best shot. We'll have to run the whole way to double our intake."

"Run?" Champ asked, chewing on a piece of candy that had fallen on the ground. "What's the use? Didn't you see the girls? They already had four buckets each!"

"Like Fisher said, we have to at least try," Pez replied.

They nodded in agreement, and Squirrel immediately took out eight more pillowcases from his backpack and handed two to each of them.

"You brought extras?" Fisher asked, impressed.

"Always be prepared," Squirrel said with a smirk. "I even packed an extra ghost sheet in my pack in case you need it."

"When did you even have time to do that?" Fisher asked.

"I have my ways," Squirrel replied, then flung the backpack over his shoulders.

The four of them ran to the next house, and the next, until they had gone all the way down the street. They took a shortcut over the Keeners' backyard fence and cut over to Hidden Oaks

Street, where there were seven big-bar houses marked on the map.

But when they turned the corner, something stopped them in their tracks.

Looming before them like a cryptic creature that had crawled out of the depths of the earth stood . . .

An abandoned mansion.

Its windows were boarded up, and the roof was missing half its shingles, like a dragon that had shed most of its scales. Creepiest of all, its gables looked like raised eyebrows gazing back at them . . . watching.

"Let's get out of here," Squirrel said. "Before the witch sees us."

5

JUST TAKE ONE

"Witch?" Fisher asked.

"Yeah, see all those bicycles bolted to the fence?" Champ said. "Those belonged to the kids she ate. She put the bikes out as a warning for the rest of us to stay away."

"Sounds like an urban legend." Fisher called Champ's bluff.

Pez shook his head. "The woman who lived here was a recluse. She never gave out treats on Halloween, so kids used to play tricks on her."

"Like what?"

"Throwing eggs at her house. Wrapping her

trees with toilet paper. That kind of thing," Pez explained.

Champ stepped forward.

"But it gets worse. One night, after scaring away some trick-or-treaters who tried to spray-paint her front door, she went back into her house and was never seen again."

"What happened to her?"

"No one knows for sure. Everyone suspected she died, but no one ever found her body."

"But they did find something disturbing up in the attic," Squirrel added.

"What?" Fisher asked nervously.

"Tiny piles of bones," Champ continued. "They thought it was the bones of cats or animals that had gotten trapped up there. But when they tested them, they found that they were the bones of children."

Fisher gulped.

"And ever since, people say when they're standing near the property, it sometimes feels like they're being pinched. It's believed to be the ghosts of all the kids trapped here," Pez finished.

Just then, Fisher felt something pinch his leg. But when he looked down, no one was there.

A ghost kid! he thought in terror. His body tensed, and goose bumps erupted all over his skin.

"Gotcha!" Champ called out, waving his arm from the chest of his tuxedo. He had snuck his hand behind Fisher and pinched his calf.

"Not funny," Fisher said.

The boys laughed in the soft glow of the streetlamp.

"So, is this whole thing some kind of initiation prank?" Fisher asked.

"No. There really is a warning in the Halloweener Diary from a long time ago that says to stay away from this place," Pez assured him.

"Especially on Halloween," Squirrel added, pointing to the black "X" he had drawn onto the map in the place where the house stood.

There was a long moment of silence. Fisher

stared up at the haunted mansion, debating whether the story was real or legend.

"If no one lives here, then what's that?"

Fisher pointed to the dilapidated front porch. Their gazes followed his finger to a black cauldron sitting on the corner, full of some kind of unidentifiable candy.

"But how?" Squirrel asked, frustrated that there wasn't a logical explanation. "No one's lived here in like thirty years."

"Maybe the witch put it there—for us," Pez said with visions of glory in his eyes.

He headed toward the porch, but Fisher grabbed his arm.

"Wait!" Fisher cautioned. "What if the candy's poisoned? What if it's part of the witch's revenge—for all the kids who used to bully her?"

"You don't have to go if you don't want to," Pez said, pulling his webbed hand away and walking up the sidewalk. He called over his shoulder, "But I don't like to lose."

"Yeah, we need the points," Champ said,

then patted Fisher's shoulder as if to say, *I'm sorry, buddy.* Then he too followed after Pez.

"But what about the warning in the Halloweener Diary?" Fisher asked.

Squirrel tapped his foot nervously. He checked his watch, then said with reluctance, "I'm going to regret this."

Fisher watched as Squirrel joined the raid too.

If I'm going to be a Halloweener, I need to act like one, Fisher told himself.

Reluctantly, he followed after the boys. When he arrived on the porch, the rotted wood creaked beneath his feet, like a ship rocking at sea.

The four of them stood over the black candy cauldron, examining it. It wasn't plastic like the others they had seen that night. It was cast iron, like what they imagined a real witch might use. Each candy bar was sealed in a solid black wrapper. The cryptic branding *MONSTER-BARS* was printed onto each one.

"I've never seen this kind of candy before,"

Champ said, reaching into the bowl and unwrapping a piece. "Must be something new the factory made this year."

He put it in his mouth and began to chew. The other boys watched him closely.

Suddenly, Champ's eyes filled with a strange madness and he grabbed for another piece.

"Look," Fisher warned, pointing to an index card taped to the front of the cauldron.

It read:

Just Take One!

Champ shook his head at the sight of the card.

"No way," he said. "This stuff tastes too good to just eat one."

He reached into the cauldron, grabbed half a dozen Monsterbars, and shoved them into his pillowcase. He then unwrapped another one and thrust it into his mouth.

"I thought you guys said we shouldn't raid a candy pot if there's a note with instructions,"

Fisher said, looking to the others. "Isn't that like . . . breaking the Second Sacred Law?"

"No one will see," Champ interjected, no longer seeming his usual self.

"Fisher's right," Squirrel said, then looked to Pez for a guiding voice. "If we can't play fair, then we don't deserve to win."

Pez mused over it for a moment, observing Champ's strange behavior. Then he reached down and picked up a Monsterbar. He inspected it for a moment, then took a cautious bite. And chewed.

Soon, his eyes grew wide with a gluttonous wonder. They were entranced, just like Champ's.

"Just take one piece?" Pez said playfully. "Or one . . . *handful*?"

Possessed by his craving, Pez reached into the cauldron for another Monsterbar.

"But you're breaking the rules!" Squirrel warned. "We're supposed to honor the Three Sacred Laws at all times!"

"Forget the rules," Pez said. "We have to do

whatever we have to do in order to win."

Pez reached into the basket, grabbed another bar, and tossed it into his pillowcase. Then another. And another.

Fisher and Squirrel could hardly believe their eyes. They couldn't have been more shocked if Bigfoot appeared at that very moment.

"I've never seen them like this," Squirrel said.

Fisher reminded himself that Champ had a hard time saying no to candy and that Pez hated to lose. But still, their behavior seemed beyond natural cravings.

Squirrel checked his watch again, stressed about staying on schedule.

"Come on—taste one, Squirrel," Champ encouraged, dangling an unwrapped piece in front of Squirrel's mouth. "And then we can get on our way to the festival."

Squirrel flinched away from the bewitched treat, trying to fight the temptation. But the seductive, chocolaty scent overcame him, and he devoured the bar right out of Champ's hand.

Squirrel's eyes instantly filled with dark illumination, just like the others'.

Fisher watched in disbelief as the Halloweeners began stashing handfuls of Monsterbars in their pillowcases, eating them one by one. Two by two. Three by three.

They've lost their minds, Fisher thought.

"You should really try one of these, Fisher," Squirrel said, fully converted. "They're the most amazing thing I've ever tasted."

"Maybe you guys shouldn't eat so many. I mean, won't we get disqualified if someone sees you?" Fisher said, sensing they had worse problems than whether they'd win the Halloween Games.

But they didn't seem to hear him, or to care.

"My mom always says too much of a good thing can become a bad thing," Champ said, gobbling down three bars at once. "Boy, was she wrong."

Just then, Champ used both his arms to pick up the cauldron and pour the rest of the Monsterbars into his pillowcase. Then he set the cauldron back down on the porch.

Before the others could complain that Champ had taken the last bars, the cast-iron pot mysteriously refilled itself.

"Did you guys just see that?" Fisher questioned.

But they still didn't hear him.

Squirrel and Pez tried to grab for more, but Champ slapped their hands away. They maneuvered around him and grabbed at the haunted candy. Then they filled their pillowcases until they could fill them no more.

How many bars have they eaten? Fisher wondered. *Is this some kind of test to see if I'll break the Sacred Laws of Halloween?*

Champ, Squirrel, and Pez each had two extra full pillowcases, with several dozen wrappers lying at their feet from the bars they had already eaten.

"We might just get enough points to beat the girls after all," Pez declared.

"But don't you guys think it's weird that the cauldron keeps refilling itself?" Fisher said again. "It's like . . . dark magic."

"Relax, Fish. It's Halloween. Magical things can happen," Pez proclaimed, holding up his pillowcase like a prized trophy.

As soon as he, Champ, and Squirrel could fill their pillowcases and pockets no more, the boys began walking back down the sidewalk. But by the time they were halfway to the street, they were moving at a slower pace.

Fisher watched as the Halloweeners exchanged ominous glances.

Then—

Champ doubled over in pain.

6

THE MONSTERS

Fisher stood in shock as he watched the Halloweeners heaving in agony. One by one, they each started throwing up. Thick black juices spilled from their mouths, staining their lips.

"Come on, guys. If this is supposed to be some kind of test, it's gone too far," Fisher said.

"Not—a—test," Squirrel groaned, barely able to get out the words.

Fisher squinted, still unconvinced. He glanced up at the house, then back to the boys.

"Did one of you put the trick candy cauldron

on the porch earlier?" he questioned.

"Swear—it's—not—a—prank," Pez moaned. "Feels—like—something—eating—me—from—inside—out."

"H-help—us—Fisher!" Champ cried.

That's when Fisher knew. He could see it in Champ's and Pez's eyes. Whatever they were feeling was real.

Then Pez's eyes turned black.

Solid black.

Like dark marbles.

It was as if the light that was Pez   his personality, his feelings, his spirit—had been snuffed out.

Suddenly, the fabric of Pez's costume began to change. The plastic melted into slimy skin, then fishlike scales began to form. Fisher could no longer tell where Pez's skin ended and the swamp creature's began. Then the gills in Pez's neck began to move. Inhaling. And exhaling. Like a fish out of water.

Pez let out a wailing cry: *Graaauuugghhh!*

Horrified, Fisher turned to Squirrel, who

was making a distressed gargling noise. His eyes had turned solid black too. The straight-A, predictable boy cocked his head back and bared his fangs to the sky. Only they were no longer plastic fangs. They were razor sharp. His cape, which had a store-bought appearance to it only a moment before, now shimmered black and red, like an evil phantom of the night.

He *hisssssed*!

Fisher looked around for Champ, but he was nowhere in sight. Strangely, on the ground where Champ had been standing was a top hat sitting upon a pile of clothes.

Just then, someone tackled Fisher, and he fell to the ground. He looked around and didn't see anyone, but he could hear Champ's cackling somewhere above him. Magically, a piece of candy unwrapped itself in midair and disappeared into an invisible gullet, followed by a loud belch.

Fisher peered out the eyeholes of his ghost sheet in panic. The Halloweeners were no longer wearing their homemade costumes. They had transformed into actual incarnations of their costumed fears.

There, before him, now stood . . .

A dehydrated swamp creature!

A vegetarian vampire!

And an invisible candysnatcher!

It was as if there was nothing left of Champ, Pez, and Squirrel. Their inner monsters had taken over entirely.

They circled around him, their hideous hands reaching toward his flesh, their mouths salivating with hunger. Fisher was certain they were about to make a feast out of him.

Then suddenly, as if the monsters shared a synchronized appetite, they sniffed the air together, lured by an irresistible scent. Before Fisher could say anything, his monster-fied friends ran across the street and disappeared into a swarm of trick-or-treaters.

"What just happened?" Fisher whispered aloud, wondering if he was trapped inside some twisted nightmare.

He removed his ghost sheet and tossed it

onto the grass beside him.

As he took a deep breath, his phone vibrated in his pocket. He lifted it from his jeans and read the text message from his mom:

WHERE ARE YOU?!
BE HOME IN 10 MINUTES,
OR I'M COMING TO LOOK FOR YOU!

A nightmare, he told himself. *This has to be a nightmare.*

But it was real.

7

HOLY HALLOWEEN!

Fisher stared down at the text message from his mom and turned off his phone.

If Mom figures out a way to track my phone, I'm done for, he thought. *I can't take any chances.*

His heart pounded in his chest as he tried to wrap his mind around what he had just seen. The Halloweeners—dressed in homemade costumes—had eaten a mysterious candy that transformed them into monsters. *Real* monsters!

Maybe I should have stayed home tonight, he thought, and considered running back to his house and hiding in his closet until morning.

He then glanced up at the mansion and remembered Champ's last words: "Help—us—Fisher."

A moment later, Champ's eyes had turned black and soulless. Fisher wondered if the Halloweeners even still existed somewhere inside their monster flesh.

Halloweeners watch out for each other, Fisher thought. *I know they'd try to help me if I was in their shoes.*

Fisher picked up Squirrel's backpack and looped the straps over his shoulders. He then hurried into the neighborhood, chasing after the monsters.

In the streets, he brushed shoulders with pirates and zombies, aliens and superheroes, fairies and clowns. In the yards, he passed by cackling witches and blow-up creatures shrouded in artificial fog. The entire neighborhood was a carnival of wonders, full of pumpkin smells and ghoulish marvels.

But he didn't see the monsters anywhere.

What if they've already hurt someone? he thought. *Or worse.*

Up ahead, Fisher saw a water hose snaking out from a yard and spilling onto the sidewalk. Amphibian-like footprints were stamped onto the pavement around it.

Pez! Fisher thought.

Nearby in the street, a candy bucket had been poured out, surrounded by a dozen empty wrappers.

Champ broke the Second Sacred Law of Halloween . . . again!

Then Fisher saw a half-eaten jack-o'-lantern lying on a nearby front porch. He could smell the scent of pumpkin guts heavy in the air.

And Squirrel destroyed the most sacred symbol of Halloween!

A light bulb flickered on in Fisher's mind.

Jeepers creepers! he realized. *They're being driven by the cravings of their costumes! The dehydrated swamp creature needs water, the invisible candysnatcher wants candy, and the vegetarian vampire is after fruits and vegetables!*

Terrified, Fisher followed the trail all the way up Hobble Lane until he arrived at a fire hydrant spraying out into the street.

"Where are they?" Fisher wondered.

Just then, a woman screamed a few yards up the sidewalk. She and her husband ran past Fisher, dragging their little boy in a mini DeLorean time machine.

Fisher quickly hid behind a maple tree.

"Holy Halloween!" he cried, peering in the direction from where the family had fled.

The front door of a white two-story house slowly opened on its own, as if unlocked by an invisible hand. Fisher watched as the invisible candysnatcher stepped inside, followed by the freakish silhouettes of the vegetarian vampire and the dehydrated swamp creature. Their fanged mouths salivated as their appetites drew them in, closer to what they craved.

That's when Fisher realized . . .

The Halloweeners just broke into someone's house!

8

MONSTER HOUSE

Fisher sprinted across the street, hoping to save the Halloweeners from doing anything they might regret. He crept through the front doorway and quickly hid beneath a table at the foot of the stairs, where a life-size skeleton decoration sat.

Two teenagers were sitting on a couch in the den, watching *Hocus Pocus*. Fisher assumed they were boyfriend and girlfriend, because the dark-haired boy kept trying to put his arm around the blond girl's shoulder. Her gaze was glued to the screen as she ate popcorn from a bowl, one kernel at a time.

Fisher then noticed a family photo sitting on the side table next to the couch. In it was the teenage girl with her parents and little brother, who looked a lot like . . .

Champ! Fisher realized. *He broke into his own home!*

Fisher heard water running upstairs, and looked up to see an open bathroom door where the dehydrated swamp creature was drinking out of the toilet.

Disgusting, Fisher thought. *I'm going to call Pez "poop breath" if I ever see him again!*

Glancing down the hall to the kitchen, Fisher saw the vegetarian vampire drinking ketchup right out of a bottle he had raided from the fridge.

Squirrel has probably never drunk anything straight out of the bottle in his life! I have to stop them before anyone in the house sees them, Fisher thought.

He looked around for any sign of Champ but couldn't see him anywhere. He started toward the kitchen to try to wrangle Squirrel, but quickly hid behind the couch when Champ's sister began to talk to her boyfriend.

"Is this diet popcorn?" Champ's sister asked, examining the bowl in front of her.

"I don't know—I just microwaved the stuff that was in the pantry," her boyfriend replied, slicking back the side of his hair and scooting a few inches closer to her.

"Oh my gosh, this better not be my little brother's Buttery Bliss," she said as if she'd realized she had just ingested poison. "This tastes too good to be diet."

"So, like, was your brother adopted or what?" the boyfriend asked, pointing to the family photo on the side table next to him. "Cuz you don't look anything alike."

Fisher noticed a picture of Champ's father wearing his Olympic silver medal, another of his mom in her aerobics apparel teaching a class, and a third one of his sister in a newspaper ad for the local sporting goods store. The wall seemed to be a shrine dedicated to their proudest family achievements.

But Champ wasn't even on the wall.

The boyfriend picked up the family photo from the table and continued, "I mean, he's sort of porky and dorky, if you know what I mean."

"It's just because he never stops eating," Champ's sister said. "We try to get him to go on our weekend family hikes, but he always just wants to stay home and play video games. He's not really like any of us."

I really hope Champ isn't hearing any of this, Fisher thought.

Just as Fisher began to crawl toward the hallway, there was a loud crash upstairs, like breaking glass. The teenagers on the couch flinched and looked over their shoulders toward the sound. The popcorn bowl hovered over the table in front of them and poured popcorn onto their heads. The half-empty candy boxes floated in midair too, moving slowly toward the front door.

Champ's sister screamed in horror and did an awkward somersault over the back of the couch, tumbling into Fisher.

Champ literally had to become invisible for his family to finally see him, Fisher mused, barely able to wrap his mind around the fantastical chaos he was witnessing.

At the sight of Fisher—who was technically a home invader—Champ's sister screamed again. Her boyfriend chased her out the back door, which was decorated to look like the entrance to a mausoleum. Fisher followed, only to find pieces of glass scattered all over the back porch. Champ's sister glanced up to the second story and saw the broken bathroom window. When she looked back down, she saw Pez standing in the middle of the pool, soaking up all the water.

She shrieked in terror.

"What is this, some kind of sick Halloween prank?!" she shouted at Fisher, who was now awkwardly standing behind them in the doorway.

At the sound of a threatening hiss, and the prospect of there being more than one creature, she and her boyfriend disappeared back into the house to hide. Fisher quickly ran past them toward the side of the house, only to find Mrs. Sanderson in her garden next door, swatting at Squirrel and yelling at him to stop feasting on her tomatoes. Red juices dripped from his chin as he bared his fangs at her and *hissssed* again and again!

The old woman screamed and threw her shovel at him, then ran back into her house with her hands waving over her head.

"Squirrel, you guys have to stop this! Before—"

Just then, a trick-or-treater started up the sidewalk toward the front door of Champ's house.

But it wasn't just any trick-or-treater. It was . . .

"Ava!" Fisher shouted.

He sprinted around the corner, hopped over a sprinkler, and tackled Ava into the bushes.

"Get off me, you fungus!" she said.

"There's—monsters!" Fisher warned, hardly

able to get the words out as he pointed toward the house.

She huffed angrily and sat up.

"Hey, I recognize your voice—you're that new kid. Our team already weighed in our candy and had our costumes judged, so it's too late to sabotage us. I was just trying to fill another couple buckets to enter last minute. I want to break my record from last year."

"You don't understand," Fisher said. "Champ, Pez, and Squirrel—they ate some weird candy, and they . . . transformed."

"Good for them. They could use a makeover," Ava replied. "Now, if you'll please hand me my broom, I have to get to the festival to accept my trophy."

Fisher picked the broom up from the grass and handed it to her.

She started to stand up, but . . .

Hissssss!

Squirrel now hovered over them, tomato juices still dripping from his fangs. Pez appeared from around the corner, followed by the two floating boxes of chocolates. At the sight of Ava's candy buckets, Champ dropped everything and grabbed her candy.

Ava squinted, perplexed, trying to figure out how the buckets were hovering in midair.

She attempted to jerk them back, but Squirrel lurched toward her and hissed like a snake. The swamp creature *graaahhhed* and shot thick green slime out of his nostrils and all over her face. The stench was more wretched than a skunk's, and more potent. She tensed up when she realized the slime was burning her skin.

"Disgusting, frog face!" she mumbled, peeling the slime from her mouth, nose, and eyes, so that she could breathe and see.

The monsters drew closer, and Ava observed their black eyes.

For the first time, she realized the monsters were real.

She tried to scream, but some chemical in the slime paralyzed the muscles in her face. It lasted several seconds before she could move her jaw again.

Fisher watched in terror.

Right then, the clock tower in Town Square struck ten. The gongs echoed over the neighborhood like a funeral song.

Together, the monsters turned toward the ringing bell, then rushed into the street, disappearing into the parade of costumed children heading toward the festival.

"What in the name of Halloween is going on?" Ava asked, just as confused as she was terrified. She rubbed her jaw, relieved that the slime had only caused a temporary paralysis. Some of it still dripped from her hair.

"Like I said, they ate some poisoned candy at an abandoned mansion on Burgundy Street, and—"

"On Burgundy?" Ava questioned. "You mean the witch's mansion?"

Fisher nodded.

"Everyone knows to stay away from that

house—especially on Halloween," Ava scolded.

Fisher shrugged. "After they ate the candy, they transformed into *real* monsters. And now they're tearing up the neighborhood! Who knows what they're capable of?"

"That's impossible," Ava said.

Just then, something caught Fisher's eye. On the ground. Right in front of him.

A black wrapper.

Of a Monsterbar.

"This is it. The candy that they ate," Fisher said, reaching to pick it up. "It must have fallen out of Champ's pocket."

He and Ava stared down at it curiously.

"Look, there's something written inside the wrapper," Ava said.

9

TOWN SQUARE TERROR

The warning on the wrapper read:

BEWARE!
EATING MORE THAN ONE PIECE
WILL HAVE A MONSTROUS EFFECT ON THE
CONSUMER.
THE RESULTS MUST BE CORRECTED BY
SUNRISE,
OR ELSE THE CONSUMER WILL BE DOOMED
TO REMAIN IN THEIR ALTERED FORM . . .
FOREVER!

Fisher put the wrapper in his pocket and gulped. The truth was worse than he had thought.

"Wait," Ava said, her eyes now plagued with horror. "You're telling me those geeks are real monsters? Like, *really* real?"

Fisher nodded.

"And this isn't some kind of elaborate hoax?" she asked.

"Do you really think we're capable of pulling off something like that?" Fisher said.

"Good point," she replied.

Fisher huffed.

"You guys really shouldn't have raided that candy cauldron," Ava scolded. "If anyone dies, it's on you."

Fisher suspected she was right, so he didn't argue.

Instead, he paced back and forth in front of the bushes, rubbing his forehead like a mad scientist trying to figure out the origins of the universe.

"What are we going to do?" he mused aloud.

"*We?*" Ava challenged. "There's no 'we' about it. They're *your* friends."

"But it's *your* town. Your family, friends, teachers—they're all in danger. We have to at least try to warn everyone at the festival," Fisher said.

Ava turned it over in her mind.

Finally, her cheeks puffed up, and she let out a slow breath like her head was a deflating balloon.

"Fine," she said. "I have to go to Town Square anyway to accept my trophy. But first I have to wash this stuff off—it's still burning my skin."

Ava ran over to the fire hydrant and washed off as much slime as she could, but her skin remained sticky and feverish. Then they ran to their bikes and pedaled toward Town Square.

On their way, Fisher noticed more candy wrappers and pumpkin guts scattered all over the pavement, as well as a slime-covered sewer cap pulled off in the middle of the street. The swamp creature's amphibian-like footprints led right into the hole.

Oh no, Pez has gone into the sewers! Fisher thought.

When they arrived in Town Square, Fisher looked around for any sign of the monsters.

A giant banner hung above Main Street: *Annual Halloween Festival!*

The mayor and his wife were on a nearby stage, judging costumes and jack-o'-lanterns and weighing candy bags for the Halloween Games. Fisher pretended not to notice the scoreboard showing the Pumpkinheads in first place.

Nearby, kids bobbed for apples out of wooden barrels surrounding the historic fountain. Parents and kids carved jack-o'-lanterns in the pavilion. And a dozen scarecrows holding candy buckets stood guard over the corn maze across from Town Hall.

The layout was immaculately organized and efficient. Like clockwork.

That's when Fisher noticed another couple standing onstage, gazing out over the mass of people having fun. The man looked down at his watch and then up at the clock tower, as if to make sure the two were in sync. He then made a small adjustment to his watch, just like Fisher had seen Squirrel do earlier in the tree house.

Those must be Squirrel's parents! Fisher realized. *I almost forgot—he said they're coordinating the festival. That's why everything is so perfect.*

Fisher then saw someone he'd never expected to see.

"We have to hide," he told Ava in a panic, quickly taking the spare ghost sheet from Squirrel's backpack and putting it on.

"Why?" she asked.

"Because my mom is here," he explained, pointing toward the steps of Town Hall.

She was walking through the crowd, examining each child's eyes behind their masks to see if it was him.

"Why are you so afraid of your mom?" Ava questioned.

"Because I'm supposed to be grounded— and she sort of hates Halloween," Fisher explained. "I snuck out tonight to go trick-or-treating. If she finds me, she'll kill me."

The two of them navigated through the crowd, looking for any sign of the monsters.

"Maybe they went somewhere else," Ava suggested.

"They have to be here," Fisher said. "Their trail led right to Town Square."

Just then, the mayor walked up to the microphone at the front of the stage.

"Good evening, boys and ghouls!" he addressed the crowd of young trick-or-treaters and their parents. "It's now time to announce the winners of this year's Halloween Games."

Ava smiled.

"It's trophy time," she said, already moving toward the stage.

"Ava, wait a minute," Fisher said, gripping her shoulder. "Do you smell that?"

She sniffed the air and cringed at the foul odor, killing the sweet autumn scent of pumpkins and candy.

"Sewage?" she whispered.

Fisher nodded. He looked around and pointed to the opened sewer lid in the middle of Main Street outside the barbershop.

Ava's eyes widened.

The mayor continued, "In first place this year is—"

Just then, someone in the crowd screamed.

"Hey! Someone just stole my candy!"

Then another person shouted, "Me too!"

And another, "Yeah, me too!"

Fisher heard a familiar cackling, like a crazed birthday clown, echo through the stage speakers.

Champ! Fisher thought. *His appetite is growing.*

Fisher turned to look for Champ but stumbled into someone behind him.

He peered up through the eyeholes of his ghost sheet and froze.

His mom stared down at him, like the grim reaper searching for the next soul to harvest. She glanced down at his shoes, and her eyes widened in recognition.

"Fisher?" she said.

She reached down to lift the sheet. But before she could remove it, a bone-chilling *grrraaaaagggghhhh* sounded from the stage!

10

FESTIVAL OF HORRORS

Onstage, the dehydrated swamp creature slimed the mayor's wife, who stumbled off the stage and onto a hay bale. He then picked up the mayor and threw him out into the crowd like a sack of potatoes.

The crowd gasped in horror and fled in all directions.

Fisher watched as the swamp creature jumped off the stage, guzzled up the water from the bobbing barrels, and then splashed into the historic fountain. After soaking up all the water, he shot an enormous amount of slime into the crowd, covering them with the stinging goo. Screams of pain filled the night.

After the creature ran out of ooze, the invisible candysnatcher gathered up the coins remaining at the bottom of the fountain and used them to empty the gumball machines in the nearby toy shop. He then chewed each gumball at a superhuman speed and stuck them on the ground so that they'd stick on the bottoms of people's shoes, and he even put them in people's hair.

Just as Fisher was about to run to help the innocent victims, the vegetarian vampire stampeded through the pavilion, feasting upon all the newly carved jack-o'-lanterns, gobbling up the apples from the bobbing barrels, and chomping up every corn cob in the corn maze.

All the while, Squirrel's parents watched in horror as the community event they had spent an entire year planning fell apart. They had no idea their sensible, organized son was one of the monsters behind the chaos.

Fisher glanced at his mom, who watched

the spectacle with a detached sense of horror. Knowing he didn't have much time before her attention turned back to him, he grabbed Ava's arm and escaped into the crowd.

His mom called after him, "Fisher! Come back! You don't know what you're getting into!"

There's no turning back now, he decided. *The Halloweeners—and the town—need my help.*

"Your friends are nuts!" Ava said accusingly.

"Those aren't my friends," Fisher corrected her. "Those are something else. Champ, Pez, and Squirrel are trapped somewhere inside them."

"What are we going to do?" Ava asked.

"*We?*" Fisher questioned.

"Yeah, we," Ava said. "But only because you owe me a trophy."

As the crowd fled into the nearby streets, Fisher heard an unnatural noise coming from the opposite direction. It was loud. And rhythmic. And the monsters heard it too, because they quickly stopped and perked their ears toward it.

"What's that sound?" Fisher asked.

"It sounds like . . . music," Ava said, perplexed.

In perfect synchronization, the monsters hurried away from the square and toward the edge of town, following after the music.

"Nothing's on that side of town except for—"

Ava paused and looked at Fisher.

"Except for what?" he asked, afraid of the answer.

"The high school!" she shouted. "The monsters are going to the Halloween dance!"

11

SCHOOL OF NIGHTMARES

Fisher and Ava pedaled through town, the wind whipping against their faces. The Hallows Eve moon was muffled by clouds hanging over the forest.

"What are we going to do once we catch your friends? I mean, the monsters," Ava asked, her broomstick knocking back and forth like a pendulum on the back of her bike.

"I don't know. But somehow, we have to warn everyone at the dance. The more the monsters eat, the bigger their appetites are becoming."

As they traversed through the streets, Fisher saw candy wrappers scattered all over the ground, half-eaten pumpkins on every porch, and fire hydrants spraying from every corner.

When they arrived at the high school, they dropped their bikes in the parking lot and ran toward the building. They found the side door open and the chain and lock broken into pieces on the ground.

The monsters were already inside.

Fisher and Ava hurried after them. Once inside the school, they stopped to observe the mess already left behind by the monsters.

Dozens of lockers were open, with candy wrappers and veggie snacks scattered across the floor. Several water fountains had been flooded, creating large, slick puddles. Fisher noticed claw marks ripped across an advertisement for the all-night monster marathon taped to the wall, and he shook his head at the irony.

"These guys are fast," Fisher said.

"They're usually pretty slow," Ava joked, nearly slipping in a puddle outside the boys' locker room.

Right then, at the other end of the hall, the cafeteria doors swung open as if someone, or something, had just passed through them.

"Let's split up," Fisher suggested. "I'll search the locker room, and you search the cafeteria."

He handed her a walkie-talkie. She stared down at it like it was some alien device.

"Do you know how to use it?" he asked.

"Of course I know how to use it," she said. "I . . . I just don't know how to turn it on."

Fisher smirked, then flipped the "on" switch.

"Keep it on channel nine. We can talk every thirty seconds, just so we know the other is okay."

Ava nodded, and they both understood the other was afraid.

Fisher watched as she headed down the

hallway and disappeared through the cafeteria doors. The exit sign at the end of each hall cast a soft red glow over the lockers and floor. Fisher thought it felt weird to be in a school at night all by themselves. Besides the reverberations of the music coming from the gym, it was so . . . quiet.

A few moments later, Fisher heard Ava's voice buzz over his walkie-talkie.

"I found the vampire," she whispered. "He's in the cafeteria, eating the frozen vegetables out of the deep freeze. What should I do?"

"Just keep an eye on him," Fisher called back. "Until I can think of a plan."

"You don't have a plan?" Ava questioned.

"Not yet," he admitted.

"Well, you'd better come up with something fast, Sherlock. We're already in way over our heads."

Ava clicked off.

Cautiously, Fisher crept into the boys' locker room. The showers were turned on, but the dehydrated creature was nowhere in sight. Fisher continued through a cloud of thick steam and opened the green door to the Olympic-size pool. As soon as he stepped into the pool area, he saw the creature sitting at the bottom of the deep end, absorbing all the water through his gills.

He's going to drink up the entire pool, Fisher thought, quickly hiding behind a nearby trophy case.

He glanced out the window to the football stadium. A light was on in the concession stand, and candy boxes and soda were being flung around.

And there's Champ!

Fisher soon noticed the wall above the trophy case, where a dozen framed photographs showcased the championship swim teams from the past decade. In each one, the same coach was standing with his arms crossed proudly beside his team.

That must be Pez's dad, Fisher thought,

glancing over at Pez. *No wonder Pez feels so much pressure to win at everything.*

Fisher pressed the talk button on his walkie-talkie, and informed Ava, "I found Pez—and Champ."

"Now what?" she said. "The vampire has almost finished off all the frozen fruits and vegetables. We won't be having Brussels sprouts for lunch on Monday."

Fisher looked around and noticed the metal speaker panel on the wall next to him.

"Maybe I should try talking to them," he told Ava. "Maybe Champ, Pez, and Squirrel can somehow still hear me."

He opened the panel and pushed several buttons, trying to find the one that activated the microphone that connected to the school intercom. Before Ava could reply, music began blaring over the school intercom.

The swamp creature flinched and climbed out of the pool.

"What happened?" Ava's voice called over the walkie-talkie.

"I think I hit the wrong button," Fisher said. "I was trying to find the—"

"Umm, Fisher?" Ava interrupted. "Your vampire friend is looking right at me. His ears look all weird, kind of like those wild animals on the Discovery Channel right before they attack a helpless victim."

"Uh-oh. Same with the swamp creature," Fisher replied. "But . . . I think he's just listening to the music. He's standing at the edge of the pool, staring up at the speaker."

Fisher glanced out the window, and no longer saw any movement in the concession stand. It appeared that Champ had gone off to find another candy stash.

Just then, the swamp creature exited the door on the opposite side of the pool.

Oh no! Fisher thought. *He's heading to find the music!*

Before he could warn Ava, her voice called over the walkie-talkie, "Fisher, the vampire's headed straight toward the dance. Meet me there before—"

A loud cackle jeered over the walkie-talkie.

Followed by a strange gurgling noise.

"Ava?!" Fisher yelled.

But there was no answer.

12

MONSTER MASH

As soon as Fisher stepped into the gym, he felt more afraid of the dancing teenagers than he was of the monsters. He could feel the costumed high schoolers glaring at him as he looked around for Ava. But she was nowhere in sight.

A giant banner stretched across the middle of the gym:

MHS HALLOWEEN DANCE

Onstage, a local band called the Cryptkeepers was playing Michael Jackson's "Thriller."

Behind them, the high school dance team—the Goaltenders—was dressed as zombies, doing the moves from the classic music video.

So this is what we'll do on Halloween once we're too old to go trick-or-treating? Fisher mused.

He looked around for his mom but didn't see her anywhere.

Just as Vincent Price's monologue began, Fisher felt someone tap on his shoulder.

He turned and was surprised to see . . .

"Ava!" he cried out, and hugged her. "I thought you were a goner."

She pushed him away and held up her walkie-talkie.

"The batteries died. Next time, check them before our lives depend on them," she said.

Fisher sighed, relieved. He didn't want to admit it, but he had figured she was sloshing around in the belly of the vampire at that very moment.

Right then, the door next to the bleachers opened and three grotesque silhouettes appeared. Even though Champ was invisible, he still somehow cast a shadow over the gym floor.

"There they are!" Fisher said, pointing in their direction.

The swamp creature, the vegetarian vampire, and the invisible candysnatcher peered out over the crowd, covering their ears at the sound of the loud music.

"We have to get to the stage," Fisher told Ava. "To warn everyone!"

"Looks like your friends are a step ahead of you," Ava said, pointing toward the stage. The monsters were climbing up onto it in a hurried rage.

Just as the vampire and creature were about to push over the band's speakers to stop the music, the song ended.

And a new one began.

The monsters then did something so unexpected, so strange, that Fisher was certain he was dreaming.

The monsters . . .

. . . began to dance.

They tapped their toes in unison, possessed by the music. As they hopped off the stage and swayed toward the center of the gym, the invisible candysnatcher grabbed a top hat, cane, and cloak from a freshman dressed as a magician and swung it over his shoulders. The makeshift costume floated in midair as he danced between the vampire and the creature.

"Are they . . . dancing?" Ava questioned, blinking twice to make sure her eyes weren't playing tricks on her.

"Affirmative," Fisher said, just as stunned as she was.

"What song is this anyway?" Ava asked.

"Are you kidding? It's the 'Monster Mash!'" said Fisher, who was a connoisseur of all things Halloween. "I thought you were supposed to know everything."

"Everything except obscure Halloween songs," she said. "Anyway, it looks like they like this one."

Fisher watched as the monsters shook their

heads from side to side and moved their hideous feet in synchronized motions. It looked like they had been practicing for months.

Soon, the crowd circled around them and began chanting "Mon-sters! Mon-sters! Mon-sters!" all while throwing their fists into the air.

"Wow, who are these guys?" Fisher overheard a teenage girl say nearby. She was dressed like Rey from Star Wars.

"What a great illusion," her friend, a Lady Gaga look-alike, agreed.

"Yeah, their costumes are really amazing," a third girl added.

Fisher watched as the vegetarian vampire attempted to do the Transylvania Twist, the swamp creature did the Wobblin' Goblin, and the invisible candysnatcher seemed to be doing something like the moonwalk.

The entire crowd soon joined in.

"This can't be happening," Fisher whispered.

"Denial. It's the first stage after experiencing trauma," Ava said matter-of-factly.

Then Fisher noticed something.

In the far corner of the gym.

The climbing rope.

It hung from the ceiling like a limp noodle.

His eyes brewed with revelation.

"Come on," he said to Ava. "I have an idea."

They hurried to the nearby equipment closet and sorted through balls, mats, and weights. Fisher soon found the spare climbing rope coiled up in the corner. But just as he was about to drag it out of the closet, he saw his mom enter through the door across the gym and start talking to the principal.

Fisher quickly hid in the closet, hoping his mom hadn't seen him.

She had a panicked look on her face as she spoke, and Fisher suspected she was explaining to the principal that she couldn't chaperone the dance tonight because she had to keep looking for her son. Fisher then noticed that she was the only person in the gym—and probably in the whole town—who wasn't wearing a costume.

Two teachers stepped in front of the closet and peered across the gym at his mom. Fisher overheard them.

"Can you believe she came back to town after all these years?" one teacher said to the other.

"I heard she got a divorce and had to move into her old family home," the other teacher replied.

"That's terrible," the first teacher said. "Especially after what happened."

After what happened? Fisher wondered.

Fisher watched as his mom left the gym, and part of him wanted to tell her he was okay.

"Are we going to do this or what?" Ava interrupted his trance.

"Sorry. Yeah, let's move," Fisher replied.

Together he and Ava dragged the thick climbing rope out of the closet and through the crowd to where the monsters were dancing.

"We have to at least act like we know what we're doing so that we blend in," Ava said, moving from side to side.

"But—I don't know how to dance," Fisher confessed.

"It's easy. Just move around like this," she said, then began gyrating her arms and legs like someone in a workout video.

It doesn't look like Ava has much experience with dancing either, Fisher thought. But he knew better than to say it aloud.

As they danced, they looped the rope around the monsters, pulling it tighter and tighter. Everyone watched, believing the rope to be part of the act. Just as the trap was set, Fisher felt the invisible candysnatcher's hand grip his shoulder.

"Fisher—please—help," Champ's voice pleaded from somewhere inside the monster.

Fisher didn't know whether to feel afraid or elated. Champ was still alive! But it sounded like he was in terrible pain. Lost in some inescapable nightmare.

Fisher then looked over at Pez and Squirrel and saw that their eyes were half black, half white. Their eyeballs waxed and waned like eclipsing moons.

"This song," Fisher whispered to Ava. "It's . . . freeing them."

"Huh?" Ava said.

But just as he and Ava were about to tighten the knot . . .

The song ended.

The monsters stopped dancing.

And their eyes turned solid black once again.

13

MIDNIGHT MAYHEM

Fisher and Ava felt the tension in the rope slackening as the monsters twisted their way out of it.

"Play the song again!" Ava shouted to the lead singer of the Cryptkeepers.

"Yeah. And hurry!" Fisher added.

But the applause was so loud, no one could hear them.

Just as the cheering subsided, the swamp creature raised his webbed hands and *grr-raaaaagggghhhhed!* Slime shot out of his nostrils, spraying the crowd with the green, skunk-like sludge that appeared to glow in the dark. The slimed victims screamed in pain.

The invisible candysnatcher tossed off his cloak and top hat, then disappeared into the crowd, cackling like a madman.

When a teenage girl dressed up like a banana ran past them, the vegetarian vampire lunged toward her and bit her arm, his razor-sharp fangs boring into her flesh. Red liquid oozed from the bite, staining the yellow fabric.

At the sight of blood, the vegetarian vampire spat in repulsion, and the teenagers surrounding the girl screamed and ran away.

"Everyone needs to get out of here now!" Fisher commanded. "Before—"

The vampire bit another teenager wearing a pumpkin costume, and more blood dripped onto the gym floor.

Their appetites are getting worse! Fisher thought.

Then . . .

Blue, flickering lights bathed the walls and ceiling.

Fisher looked out the windows behind the bleachers and saw two police cars pulling up outside. A moment later, two cops entered the gym, their hands readied on their holsters.

The swarm of teenagers stampeded in every direction, whirling past the cops.

"Can someone please tell us what's going on here?" a man in a state trooper uniform yelled. "We had a call about a—"

Before he could finish, his hat flew off his head, swatted by an invisible hand. Champ's mischievous laughter soon followed.

"What the—" the cop began, then tripped over his shoelaces, which the invisible candy-snatcher had tied together.

"Look!" Ava shouted. "They're getting away!"

The monsters pushed the speakers off the stage, shattering them to pieces. Then they escaped out the back door of the gym, slipping into the October night once again.

Fisher and Ava hurried after them.

As soon as Fisher stepped outside, he saw

the monsters disappear into the woods behind the football stadium.

A third cop car pulled up, and Fisher and Ava quickly hid behind the nearby bushes.

They could overhear the conversation taking place on the CB radio. . . .

The dispatcher at the police station buzzed through. "Officer Copeland, we've just received a report for a missing child. He's wearing black air-pump Jordans and a white ghost sheet. His mom has called into the station about ten times, so we need to find him and get him home before she calls in the federal troops."

Officer Copeland, whose bald head gleamed in the moonlight, picked up the receiver and replied, "I've seen a dozen kids in ghost sheets tonight, Marla. You're asking me to find a needle in a haystack."

"The chief wants you on it immediately," Marla called back. "We've got weirder problems down here at the station. We're getting reports of mutated creatures drinking out of swimming pools and eating up gardens. We even had one guy call in about an invisible burglar! I really hate Halloween."

"Roger that. I'm on it," Officer Copeland said, then chomped another bite of his doughnut.

As soon as he drove out of sight, Fisher confessed to Ava, "I'm the missing kid they're looking for."

"If it makes you feel any better, at least your mom is out looking for you," Ava said. "My parents probably haven't even noticed I'm gone. They're out at a masquerade party with their rich friends tonight."

Then she patted Fisher's shoulder. The gesture wasn't patronizing like usual. It was sincere, as if she was just trying to say, *It's okay*.

"By the way, thanks for saving us back there," she added.

"No problem," Fisher replied, surprised by Ava's change of persona. "Did you see all the blood on the gym floor? This is getting way serious."

"We have to make a plan. *Now*," she said.

"The warning on the candy wrapper said we have to reverse the curse before sunrise. It's already past ten o'clock."

Fisher glanced toward the forest. The trees waved gently in the breeze. They seemed more haunted than ever.

"I know a place where we might be able to find the answers we need," Fisher said. "But it's sort of secret. So you can't tell anyone if I take you. Swear?"

"I swear," Ava said. "But we have to hurry."

They ran toward their bikes, which were still lying in the parking lot. They hopped on and darted back into the night.

We're the town's only hope, they both thought, but neither said it aloud.

14

MAKING A PLAN

As soon as they arrived at the base of the tree house, Fisher blindfolded Ava.

"You already showed me how to get here, so why does it matter if I can see now?"

"It will just make me feel better," Fisher said.

He tightened the blindfold over Ava's eyes, then pulled the secret rope in the tree hollow for the ladder to fall down. He led her up, rung by rung, and through the door at the bottom of the fort.

Once inside, he lit a kerosene lantern. The walls came alive with posters of werewolves and vampires, witches and robots, swamp creatures and zombies.

Ava looked around. "So this is the secret hideout of the Halloweeners?" she said, running her fingers over each cryptic drawing pinned to the wooden planks. "Impressive. I'll have to remember to trash this place next time you guys toilet paper my house."

"You promised you wouldn't tell anyone I brought you here," Fisher reminded her. "If you do, I'll—"

"You'll what?" she challenged him.

"I'll tell everyone you tried to kiss me."

"Gross!" Ava shouted. "Like anyone would believe you."

"Just don't tell anyone, okay? They won't let me in the club if they find out I brought you here," Fisher urged.

"All right, all right, I was just kidding," Ava said. "But if they ever turn back into their normal selves, I'm sure they'll understand this was an emergency. Anyway, must be nice to have friends like that."

"But . . . you have plenty of friends," Fisher said.

Ava shook her head.

"Those girls you saw me with tonight—they only hang out with me because my parents are rich. I mean, one time I had an argument with my mom, and I called Ginger to talk about it. Ginger said she was busy and would call me back later but never did. She didn't even ask me about it the next day at school. And another time, I invited them to come to my piano recital, and they all made up excuses about why they couldn't be there. The next week they all showed up to my birthday party two hours late just so they could get the party favors and a piece of cake my mom ordered from a luxurious bakery, then they left."

"But Champ said you guys win the Halloween Games every year. You're a team. So you have to at least sort of be friends, right?"

"There's a difference between competing together and being friends," Ava corrected him. "And my parents don't have much time for me either, so I'm sort of on my own."

Fisher suddenly realized that he and Ava had something unexpected in common—they both needed friends. Real friends.

Ava approached a drawing on the wall of a green monster with electrodes sticking out of its neck.

"Hey, you guys know that Frankenstein isn't the name of the monster, don't you? It's the name of the scientist who created the monster," Ava pointed out, back to her usual annoyingly clever self.

"Of course I knew that," Fisher replied, sure that he had read it somewhere.

He fumbled through the bookshelves, looking for something.

Finally, he pulled a worn leather book from the bottom shelf. A small plastic contraption hung from a ribbon in the middle of the book. It looked like a square magnifying glass, only much smaller. And the lens was yellowish instead of clear.

"What is that?" Ava asked.

"I think it's the Halloweener Diary," he explained. "I heard the guys talking about it earlier. Supposedly, it holds all their secrets. And this little thing attached to it must be some kind of cypher."

Fisher opened the worn leather journal. He turned the pages until he arrived at a series of handmade illustrations. The heading read:

How to Kill Monsters

"This may be just what we need," Fisher said.

"So . . . you want us to kill your friends?" Ava asked dryly.

"No. But if we can figure out a way to destroy the monster side of them, then maybe we can save the *real* them."

Ava squinted, considering Fisher's plan.

"Sounds tricky. And dangerous."

"Do you have a better idea?" Fisher asked.

Ava was silent.

"Look," he continued, pointing to a drawing

of garlic melting a vampire's face. He held the cypher up to it, and calligraphic words like those of an ancient monster hunter appeared beneath it:

Garlic will repel vampire energy.
A stake through its heart will destroy it forever.

"We need garlic," Fisher said.

"And a stake," Ava added, pointing to a wooden stake going through the vampire's heart. "But what about the dehydrated swamp creature?"

She pointed to an illustration of a mutated beast covered in toxic slime and crawling out of a lake. It then showed the creature lying lifelessly in the sun, with its dried tongue hanging out the side of its mouth and all its scales peeling off.

He held up the cypher, and more words appeared.

"Death by dehydration," Fisher whispered.

"Pez is already dehydrated. But we need to finish him off."

"With what? We can't wait until the sun comes out," Ava said.

Fisher thought for a moment, then whispered, "Soda."

"Soda?"

"Yeah, sugar and caffeine dehydrate a water-based body," Fisher explained. "I learned it at summer camp."

"And what about the invisible candy-stealer kid?"

Fisher perused the diary for any mention of invisibility.

"There's not anything here about how to defeat an invisible monster," Fisher said. "Maybe we can throw paint on him so that he becomes visible. People will see him coming, so he won't be able to cause mischief or steal things as easily. At least until we can find a way to reverse the curse permanently."

"You're not as dumb as you look," Ava said with a smirk.

"Thanks," Fisher replied, unsure if he should feel flattered or offended.

"What's this?" Ava asked, moving the cypher to the bottom of the page.

A cryptic message read:

Monsters are considered to be part of the animal kingdom.

Therefore, their senses are . . .

But the corner of the page was torn off, and they couldn't read the rest.

"I wonder what the missing part says," Fisher mused aloud, then looked out at the moonlit graveyard. "We have to hurry. Before the monsters hurt anyone else."

He unzipped Squirrel's backpack and shoved the diary inside it. Then he took a Super Soaker water gun from the nearby couch and put it in the pack as well.

"Food Mart will have everything else we need," he said.

"Great idea!" Ava agreed.

They climbed back down the tree to their bikes, rode past the graveyard, and soared into town.

"Garlic, soda, paint. Garlic, soda, paint," Fisher repeated over and over again all the way to Food Mart.

But when they arrived in the parking lot, the windows were all shattered, the lights were flickering, and strange sounds were coming from inside.

"The monsters," Ava whispered. "They're already here!"

15

EAT YOUR HEART OUT

Fisher and Ava stepped up to the sliding doors of Food Mart, activating the motion sensors. They crept inside, shocked by the postapocalyptic appearance of their local grocery store. The lights blinked on and off, buzzing like a swarm of Amazonian insects. Shelves were turned over. Food boxes were scattered across the floor. Fisher felt like he was walking through a scene in a horror film.

"Look," Ava whispered, pointing to the produce section.

It had been ransacked, with fruits and

vegetables thrown everywhere. Only a few cores, stems, and pits remained. Fisher picked up a stray clove of garlic and put it in his pocket.

"We need to get the supplies before the monsters see us," he urged.

"Yeah, or eat us," Ava added.

"I'll get the soda. You get the paint," Fisher said.

Ava nodded, and the two of them headed off to find their monster-hunting essentials.

Fisher crept cautiously across the slick floor, careful not to make a screeching sound with his sneakers.

When he turned onto the soda aisle, he saw the swamp creature at the other end, gulping down gallons of purified water. Dozens of empty jugs already lay on the floor.

Fisher quietly pulled the Super Soaker from his backpack and reached for a liter of Dr Pepper. When he twisted off the cap, the compressed carbonation made a harsh hissing sound.

The swamp creature dropped his water jug and turned to Fisher.

"Oh no," he whispered, pouring soda into the Super Soaker as fast as he could.

Then—

The creature began running toward him.

Like a madman, Fisher pumped streams of soda at it. The carbonated liquid hissed like acid against its scaly skin. Smoke arose upon impact, and the creature grabbed at its own flesh, squealing in pain.

Soon, it fell to its knees.

"It's working," Fisher said, quickly reloading with another liter of Dr Pepper.

He shot the next round of soda at the creature, soaking its chest and head. Fisher could see its skin growing dryer. And grayer. The creature was dying.

Soon, it lay lifeless on the ground.

Fisher sprayed one last jet of soda onto its chest. Victoriously.

"Pez, are you in there? Can you hear me?" But there was no reply.

With no time to waste, Fisher quickly ran to find Ava.

When he turned the corner onto the canned foods aisle, he saw the vegetarian vampire holding Ava by her neck high up in the air. Her feet were dangling, trying to find the floor. Empty cans of fruits, vegetables, and lentils were scattered everywhere.

"Let her go!" Fisher yelled, holding up the garlic clove as he ran at the vampire. But the vampire grabbed Fisher's wrist, plucked the garlic right out of his hand, and devoured it in a single gulp.

Fisher quickly looked around for more ammunition, and then ran to the nearby meat section. He tore open a package of uncooked steaks and grabbed a slimy red rib eye.

"What—are—you—doing?" Ava managed to get out the words, her face turning blue from lack of air.

"The chart in the tree house said that a *stake* through the heart could destroy a vampire," Fisher reminded her.

"But—those—are—two—different—things," Ava corrected him, barely able to speak.

"One's—a—piece—of—meat—and—the—other's—a—piece—of—wood."

"A stake's a steak," Fisher said with a shrug, then held up the piece of meat in front of the vampire's face. "Eat your heart out, vamp!"

He shoved the steak against the vampire's cheek, and the meaty juices soaked into his pale skin, searing his flesh. The vampire screamed like a madman and dropped Ava to the ground.

"I told you it would work," Fisher called over to her. "Meat is a vegetarian's Kryptonite."

"Now, if we could only get him to eat it, he might die of a heart attack," Ava added.

"Good idea. We need to remember that," Fisher agreed.

Right then, the mischievous candysnatcher tried to set Ava's hair on fire with a lighter.

She grabbed the nearby bucket of blue paint she had already retrieved, popped off the lid, and hurled the thick liquid in the direction of the invisible boy. Two blue legs instantly appeared out of thin air.

"We can see him now!" she proclaimed as

the candysnatcher's lighter fell to the ground, igniting the pool of paint. A trail of fire followed the invisible boy, who quickly ran down the cereal aisle to hide.

"Uh-oh," Fisher said, looking at the growing flames.

A moment later, the ceiling sprinklers turned on, showering the entire store.

"The swamp creature!" Fisher remembered, glancing up at the water spraying down on them. He and Ava ran back to the soda aisle just in time to see the invisible candysnatcher slurping soda off the ground around the swamp creature's body.

The endless churning of water showered down upon the creature, revitalizing its rubbery flesh with color and new scales. Its arms moved, then its legs, then its gills. It slowly rose from the floor like a zombie from its grave and *graaahhhed* with fury.

Fisher heard the *hisssss* of the vampire a few aisles over and the cackling of the candysnatcher running off to another aisle. Then, as if they were all synchronized, the three monsters rushed toward the front of the store at once and disappeared out of Food Mart.

"They're running away from town," Ava said. "Where could they possibly be going now?"

Fisher's eyes grew wide as he saw the soft light of a giant movie screen in the near distance, next to the town water tower.

"To the drive-in movie theater," he whispered.

"Oh no!" Ava said.

16

MONSTER MARATHON

The marquee outside the drive-in movie theater read:

ALL-NIGHT MONSTER MARATHON!
SPONSORED BY BUGFRY CANDY
FACTORY!
EVERYONE'S INVITED!

We're already living inside a monster marathon, Fisher thought as he and Ava rode past the ticket booth, nearly waking up Mr. Palmer, whose family had owned the place for almost seventy years.

There were at least a hundred cars in the lot—mostly families and teenage couples. Nearby, a dozen food trucks were set up with corn dogs, funnel cakes, and corn on the cob. The entire area was twice as crowded as Town Square had been earlier in the evening. Best of all, *Ghostbusters* was playing on the giant drive-in screen.

"What time is it?" Fisher asked.

Ava glanced at her watch.

"Almost three a.m. We don't have much time."

Just then, two younger boys walked past them. Fisher and Ava overheard their conversation. . . .

"Can you believe the Candy Factory ran out of candy tonight?" a boy dressed like a zombie said.

"It's never happened before. They should have made more candy," his friend, a cowboy, said.

Fisher glanced at the nearby candy truck, where a mass of disappointed customers were walking away after being told the news.

"How in the world could the candy factory run out of candy on Halloween?" Ava asked.

Fisher's eyes grew wide, and he pointed to the car in front of them. "Champ!"

Just then, a half-eaten candy bar hovered out of the open window. Then another. And another.

In the cornfield next to the drive-in, Fisher saw shucks being tossed up in the air like candy at a parade. Whatever was eating them was coming right toward the drive-in. Soon, countless screams emanated from Old Joe's Pumpkin Farm next door.

"Squirrel!" Fisher whispered. "He's eating the entire corn field—and all the pumpkins! But where's Pez?"

Right then, Ava's gaze slowly ascended above the trees, and her mouth fell open as if she were looking at a UFO.

"Oh. My. Gosh."

Fisher glanced up to see the swamp creature standing on top of the water tower on the other side of the drive-in fence. He looked like a giant lizard silhouetted against the moon as he tried to break into the town water supply, drinking out of a leaky hole he had made with his talons.

Once revitalized, the creature leaped from the slide and landed on top of the drive-in screen. People peered out their car windows at the strange form, trying to figure out what it was.

The swamp creature threw back its head and hawked an unfathomable amount of slime through its nostrils, splattering green ooze onto every windshield and hood in the lot.

Screams echoed out of the car windows.

Meanwhile, the vegetarian vampire jumped onto the hood of a truck, shattering its slime-covered windshield. He squeezed packets of ketchup into his mouth, and the red goo dripped from his fangs like blood.

The teenage girl in the passenger seat screamed, and her panicked boyfriend tried to start the car. Other headlights turned on as families and couples attempted to escape. But every tire in the lot was flat, every battery was dead, and every gas gauge was on empty.

A mischievous cackling echoed in the night as the invisible candysnatcher finished sabotaging every car, truck, and minivan in the lot.

"This is madness!" Ava declared as the crowd ran from their cars back toward town, some hardly able to move because of the paralyzing slime. A few kids were stuck lying in the dirt, unable to move until the numbing effect wore off.

Soon, all three monsters stepped in front of the projector beam, their ghastly silhouettes cast against the movie screen.

Fisher turned to Ava. "Remember what you said back at Food Mart about giving the vampire a heart attack?"

"Yeah," Ava replied.

"Well, I have an idea," Fisher said, handing the backpack to her. "Don't do anything until I say so. Okay?"

Ava nodded, understanding his plan.

Fisher crept around the side of the projector house and cautiously confronted the monsters.

"Champ? Pez? Squirrel? I know you guys are in there somewhere," he began. "If you can hear me, you have to find a way to help us beat the monsters."

The vegetarian vampire hissed. The swamp creature growled. And the invisible candy-snatcher laughed wildly, then threw a handful of Reese's Pieces at Fisher's face.

Drool dripped from their mouths as they closed in on him from all sides.

Closer.

And closer.

"I'm warning you guys," Fisher said, but they kept drawing nearer. And nearer. Finally, he shouted, "Now, Ava!"

The monsters exchanged confused glances.

Ava appeared around the corner, holding up two raw steaks Fisher had hidden in the backpack.

"Meat thy doom!" she yelled, then shoved

the two rib eyes into the vegetarian vampire's mouth.

The vampire howled in pain as the steak juices singed his tongue and cheeks.

Ava lifted the Super Soaker and sprayed the dehydrated creature with a stream of acidic soda. Within five seconds, half of the creature's new scales had disintegrated into dust.

But then the stream of soda disappeared into thin air.

The invisible candysnatcher is drinking it! Fisher realized.

"I'm out of soda!" Ava shouted.

"Hurry and reload!" Fisher called back, pointing to the backpack.

While Ava hurried to pour more soda into the Super Soaker, the vampire coughed up the steaks. The swamp creature turned on the nearby hose attached to the projector house and poured it over his own body, rejuvenating his scales. And the invisible candysnatcher laughed victoriously.

The monsters were undefeatable.

Suddenly, the vampire grabbed Fisher's neck and threw him to the ground. The monsters loomed over him like a nightmare gang, their eyes as black as night.

Fisher realized in that moment that the Halloweeners—the revered protectors of Halloween—no longer existed. Only the monsters remained. And they were about to destroy him.

Ava stood nearby, watching helplessly. She knew they would get her next.

At the sight of the vampire fangs bearing down on him, Fisher closed his eyes. And waited for the sting of death.

But right then, something unexpected happened. . . .

Pffffpphhh!!!!!

An air horn shrieked from behind the monsters.

They covered their ears, turning toward the unbearable sound, and fell to their knees in agony.

Of course! Fisher thought. *Monsters are technically part of the animal kingdom; therefore their senses are heightened! That was the missing piece of the diary! And that's why they were trying to destroy the speakers at the dance!*

The monsters began to run, stumbling over one another. Fisher watched them disappear around the corner, then glanced in the direction from which the air horn had blown. The light from the projector blinded him, and he put his hand in front of him so he could see the face of his rescuer.

Cold, stinging fear rushed over him as he laid eyes on the scariest monster he had seen all night. . . .

"Mom?"

17

MOTHER KNOWS BEST

Fisher's mom didn't say a word the entire drive home. Fisher sat peering out the window at the chaos. . . .

Hydrants spewed from every corner. Half-eaten jack-o'-lanterns were smeared upon moonlit sidewalks. And candy wrappers were scattered across lawns like fallen leaves.

His mom had figured out a way to track his phone even with it turned off, and had followed the homing device all the way to the drive-in. They hadn't been able to get ahold of Ava's parents, so they had dropped her off at her house on the way home. Fisher imagined she was sitting in her room at that very moment, wondering if the past six hours had really happened.

As soon as Fisher and his mom stepped inside their home, she dead-bolted the front door. And then every other door in the house.

"They've evacuated all the streets in town and are warning everyone to stay inside until they can figure out what's going on," she explained.

She began taping cardboard over the windows so that no one could see inside. Then she reached for garlic in the pantry but hesitated.

"You said the vampire is a vegetarian?" she asked.

Fisher examined her face to see if she was joking, but her eyes were deadly serious. He nodded.

She grabbed raw steaks from the fridge and set them at every door.

"And the swamp creature has a water-based body?"

Fisher nodded again.

His mom went to the utility room and turned off all their water.

She's monster-proofing the house, Fisher realized, surprised that his mom knew how to do such a thing.

"You sneaking out tonight is exactly why I don't care for Halloween," she said, filling up his Super Soaker with green paint in order to spray any invisible trespassers. "It's a bad influence on kids."

"Mom, I shouldn't have gone out without letting you know where I was," Fisher apologized. "But I knew you wouldn't let me go, and those guys were trying to be my friends. Ever since the divorce, you haven't listened to—"

"Enough about the divorce, Fisher," she said. "You think you're the only one it's been hard on? Try being a single parent."

You never care about how I feel! Fisher thought, but he didn't think it would do any good to say it aloud.

His mom continued, "You disobeyed, and now you're grounded until we move. You can make new friends at your new school. For now, we need to focus on getting the house packed up."

Fisher thought of Champ, Pez, and Squirrel. He wanted *them* to be his friends. And he knew they still needed him.

"Mom, I need to tell you something," he began. "There was this weird candy at a house we went to tonight, and my friends—the Halloweeners—they turned into monsters. They're the ones you saved me from at the drive-in."

She stared at him curiously, and he couldn't tell if she understood what he was saying.

"The Halloweeners?" she said, as if she thought it was a strange word.

"Yeah," Fisher confirmed.

"You shouldn't get mixed up with that sort" was all she replied; then she walked into the hallway.

She pulled down the attic door and lowered the retractable ladder to the floor.

"Up!" she commanded, motioning for Fisher

to climb the ladder.

"You want me to go up in the attic?" he said. "By myself?"

She held out a flashlight and took a sleeping bag out of the closet.

"You'll sleep up there tonight until everything is under control," she said. "There are no windows up there. And no doors. So you'll be safe."

He understood the real reason, though. She was sending him to a prison cell with no escape. He would be locked up there all night while his friends were tasered, captured, or killed by a mob.

"Now!" his mom urged. "Don't make me ask again."

Fisher hung his head low and took the flashlight and sleeping bag from her. He stepped onto the first rung of the ladder.

"I just have one question," he called over his shoulder.

"What is it?"

"The air horn. How did you know it would

scare away the monsters?"

"I didn't," she said. "But it's all I had in the car."

"Oh," he said, secretly wishing there was a more mysterious reason why she knew.

Fisher nodded and disappeared into the attic. He wanted to ask her about what he had overheard the teachers saying in the gym and tell her about everything he had experienced that night. But his mom closed the door, shutting him away in the darkness. He could hear her footsteps below, probably booby-trapping the house for invisible trespassers.

How does someone who hates Halloween know so much about monsters? he wondered.

18

ATTIC SECRETS

The dusty beam of the flashlight licked the walls, illumining cobwebbed rafters and forgotten memories. Fisher walked past a stack of boxes, a grimy mirror, and a broken wardrobe, then ran his finger over an old rocking horse. He knew his mom had grown up in that same house, and he wondered if all these artifacts had been left behind by family members he had never known.

Soon, something caught his eye.

Behind the mirror.

Tucked away in the darkest corner of the attic.

"An old wooden trunk?" he whispered.

Black and orange streamers hung out of it like tentacles, and for a moment, Fisher thought there might be something living inside it.

He pulled on the rusted lock until it broke, then he lifted the brass clamp. When he shined his flashlight inside the trunk, he was surprised by what he found. . . .

A witch's hat.

Several tiny skeletons.

And a battery-powered ghost.

What are all these things doing up here? he wondered. *Mom never decorates for Halloween.*

He lifted a leather scrapbook from the trunk and dusted off its cover.

When he opened to the first page, he saw a picture of a little girl standing with her parents. They were all dressed up like the Addams Family.

"Great Halloween costumes," he whispered.

He turned through the pages and saw the same family partaking in various Halloween rituals. . . .

The girl and her father carving a jack-o'-lantern.

The girl and her mother hanging fake cobwebs in the kitchen.

The girl and her little brother scaring trick-or-treaters on their front porch.

Fisher then noticed a folded piece of construction paper glued into the scrapbook.

He unfolded it, and smiled at the girl's drawing of a haunted house. A black candy cauldron was sitting on the front porch. Playful handwriting was inscribed over it with an orange marker:

BEWARE OF THE WITCH!

And then beneath it:

PS Hallie is for Halloween!

Fisher blinked.

"Hallie?" he whispered. "But . . . that's my mom's name."

He let it sink in.

"My mom was named after Halloween? And she knows about the witch?"

He turned to the last page in the scrapbook.

A Polaroid revealed her dressed up like a green-faced witch, stirring a plastic cauldron with a group of friends. They were all wearing Halloween costumes and holding bright orange pumpkin buckets like they were about to go trick-or-treating. Not only that, but they were standing in a tree house. The very same tree house where he had just taken Ava.

The inscription beneath the photo read:

The Halloweeners,
1989.

Fisher felt his stomach churn. He closed his eyes for a moment, wondering if they were playing tricks on him. Then he glanced at the photo again, and was certain of what he was seeing.

"My mom . . . was a Halloweener?" he whispered.

19

THE HAUNTING TRUTH

It took a moment for Fisher to absorb the meaning of the photograph.

In it, the little girl—his mom—seemed so happy. She was an entirely different person from the grown-up Hallie he knew. Her friends even looked a lot like his own friends, just with different hairstyles and clothes.

If my mom was a Halloweener when she was my age, then why does she hate Halloween so much now? he wondered.

He then noticed a yellowed newspaper article buried in the bottom of the trunk. Its edges were curled, and the black ink was covered in dust. He carefully lifted it. The top was dated *November 1, 1989.*

On the front page of the article was a picture of his mother's family. His mom was about Fisher's age, standing in the front. Her mother's hands were on her shoulders, and her father's hands were on her little brother's shoulders right next to her. All of them were smiling. Happy. Loved. Together.

Fisher read the headline printed in big block letters:

HALLOWEEN HORROR:
TRAGIC ACCIDENT KILLS THREE

Fisher felt a chill splinter down his spine.

He read the article aloud to himself: "'It is suspected that the Gibbs family was searching for their daughter, who had stayed out late trick-or-treating, when their car skidded off the road near Old Joe's Pumpkin Farm. Witnesses say the car rolled three times, finally ramming into a grain silo. The three passengers were taken to the county hospital, where they later perished. They are survived by their daughter, eleven-year-old Hallie Gibbs. The funeral will be held tomorrow at Irving Chapel, and the deceased will be buried in side-by-side plots in Oakwood Cemetery. . . .'"

Fisher set down the article. He could barely breathe.

His body suddenly felt heavier than it ever had before. He had always known that something happened to his mom's family when she was younger, but he had only asked about it a few times, and his mom was always vague with her answers. Now his heart was broken, not just for his family members who had died, but for his mom. For the first time in his life, he understood her. He understood why she didn't like being in this house, or in this town.

She hates Halloween because that's the night her family died. And she thinks it was her fault, Fisher realized. *She probably thinks that if she hadn't stayed out late trick-or-treating, they never would have gone looking for her and they'd still be alive.*

Just then, something scratched against the ceiling of the attic. It sounded like critters on the roof.

Fisher jumped, certain that the monsters were outside, trying to claw their way in.

His walkie-talkie buzzed, and he pulled it out of his pocket.

"Fisher, can you hear me? Fisher, are you inside your house?"

It was Ava.

"I'm here," he called back, glad to hear her voice. "But my mom's locked me in the attic. What's going on out there?"

"The monsters are tearing up the town," she said. "Time's almost up. We have to figure out a way to reverse the curse!"

"I'm stuck in here. There's literally no way out," he said.

"Don't be so sure," she replied.

Fisher heard movement against the wall on the far side of the attic. A circular grate popped out, and he could see moonlight beaming in from outside.

"My uncle installs air conditioners," Ava said, peeking in. "I knew there had to be a vent grate that connected to the attic."

"You're a genius!" Fisher whispered, hurrying over to her. He stuffed the newspaper article into his pocket and glanced down again at his mother's drawing of the witch's house. He suddenly remembered something his mom had said earlier that night at the festival: *Fisher! Come back! You don't know what you're getting into!* She said it as if she somehow knew what the night had in store. And he wondered if his mom knew something about the witch and her cauldron.

"I know where we have to go," he said.

"Where?" Ava asked.

"We have to go back to the house where Champ, Pez, and Squirrel ate the candy. If we can figure out who put the cauldron there and why, then maybe we can figure out how to reverse the curse."

Ava and Fisher jumped off the roof and ran into the night.

What they didn't know was that one of them would be dead within the hour.

20

NOT AFRAID TO DIE

As Fisher and Ava sprinted through the streets, they observed the trail of pandemonium left behind by the monsters. Not a single person was outside—everyone was locked up safely in their houses.

Everyone except for Fisher and Ava.

"We only have an hour until sunrise," Ava said, glancing down at her watch.

"That's not enough time," Fisher fretted. "We have to stop the monsters from doing any more damage."

"I don't know how we're going to reach them

all in time," Ava replied. "I heard on the radio that they've separated across town."

Suddenly, Fisher slowed down his pace.

Ava ran a few yards ahead of him, then turned around.

"Why are you stopping? We have to hurry!" she implored.

Fisher stared down at the ground, pondering something.

"You saw how the monsters reacted to the air horn back at the drive-in, didn't you?"

"Yeah. So?"

"The sound paralyzed them because they have heightened senses. I think that was the missing piece of the diary, and also why they were trying to destroy the speakers back at the dance. If we can re-create that noise on a larger scale, then maybe we can stop them from causing any more damage until we can figure out how to reverse the spell."

"How are we going to do that?"

Fisher turned in a circle, perusing the horizon. His eyebrows soon rose with an idea.

"Does this town have a storm siren?" he asked.

"You mean like for hurricanes and tornadoes?" Ava questioned, intrigued.

"Yeah."

She thought for a moment, then pointed toward Town Square.

"There's one on top of Town Hall."

"Good! If we can figure out a way to turn it on, then maybe we can hold off the monsters."

"But we'd need a key or ladder or something to get up on the roof—and we don't have any time," Ava reminded him.

"Unless . . ." Fisher glanced down at Ava's broom.

"Why are you looking at me like that?" Ava questioned.

Fisher smiled.

"Come on," he said, and grabbed her hand. "I have an idea."

They ran another two blocks until they arrived at the overgrown lot where the abandoned mansion sat. It seemed even scarier in the middle of the night, when no one else was out in the neighborhood.

"I've spent every Halloween of my life avoiding this place," Ava said.

"Well, you can't stay away from it any longer," Fisher said, then led her up the sidewalk.

As they approached the front porch, Fisher saw the pillowcases and candy in the yard from earlier that night. His original ghost sheet was still lying in the grass right where he had left it.

They stepped up to the front door, and Fisher ran his fingers over the cracked wood and faded paint.

Whiiissshh!

A cold wind brushed over them, like the icy breath of Death.

Moonlight poured through the clouds above and illumined the candy cauldron beside them. No other part of the porch was touched by the moonlight—only the pot.

Fisher squatted down beside it.

"The Halloweeners ate at least ten pieces each, and their eyes turned solid black. Maybe if you just eat two or three, you'll change, but still have control over your mind," he presented.

"Change?!" Ava cried. "I'm not eating that stuff!"

"Do you want to save the town?" Fisher said.

He started to unwrap a bar to give to Ava, and accidentally knocked over the "Just Take One" card. It fell beside him, and he noticed a mysterious message written on the back of it:

IF A CONSUMER EATS MORE THAN JUST ONE PIECE,
*   THE ONLY WAY TO REVERSE THE CURSE*
*   IS TO WORK A MONSTROUS MIRACLE*.*
*   ONLY THEN MAY BALANCE RETURN TO THE WORLD.*

"Monstrous miracle?" Fisher whispered, and he and Ava exchanged a curious glance. "Like what?"

Ava pointed to more words that were in fine print at the bottom of the card:

*MONSTROUS MIRACLES INCLUDE,
BUT ARE NOT LIMITED TO:
RESURRECTING THE DEAD,
CONJURING A FULL MOON,
OR FREEING A HAUNTED HEART.

Fisher stared down at the card, its ink glimmering in the moonlight.

"A haunted heart?" he whispered.

Something about it sounded familiar.

Then it hit him like a lightning bolt. "Like . . . my mom! She has a haunted heart!"

He thought of how creeped out he had been by the graveyard earlier that afternoon, and he remembered the rusted sign above the iron gates, *Oakwood Cemetery*. The article he had found in the attic said his mother's family had been buried there in side-by-side plots.

If I can find their graves, maybe I can talk

to them, he realized. *After all, tonight's the only night of the year when the Dead wander among the Living.*

He took out the Halloweener Diary and skimmed through the pages looking for any entries about ghosts. Finally, he found one written in bolded letters:

> *In order to awaken a sleeping spirit,*
> *One must place a jack-o'-lantern atop a grave on Hallows' Eve,*
> *But beware, the Living will be deaf, mute, and blind to the conjured soul,*
> *For only the Dead can speak to the Dead.*

"Only the Dead can speak to the Dead," Fisher whispered.

He glanced over at his ghost sheet lying in the yard, and his eyes widened with an idea—a terrible, impossible, fantastical idea!

Fisher turned to Ava, who stood watching him anxiously.

"I think I know what I have to do," he said.

He ran to the yard and grabbed the ghost sheet, then returned to the porch.

"Once you eat a few of these, you'll turn into a real witch, and you can fly to the storm siren. But you have to control your appetite—don't eat more than two or three, okay?" he said.

"Are you crazy?" Ava challenged. "I'm afraid of flying, remember?"

"Just trust me," he encouraged her, then looked down at the cauldron full of Monsterbars. "I have something else I have to do."

With no other choice in sight, he put on the ghost sheet.

Fisher unwrapped three Monsterbars and shoved them into his mouth. He chewed swiftly, and their sweet juices flowed over his tongue.

Admittedly, it was the best candy he had ever tasted in his entire life.

"Are you sure this is safe?" Ava questioned. But her voice seemed so far away.

He stood and examined his hands peeking out from under the ghost sheet. They were still made of flesh and blood.

"It's not working," he told Ava in surrender, while fighting his craving to eat another bar.

As she followed Fisher back down the sidewalk, his stomach started to feel strange, but nothing like the violent pain his friends had suffered after they ate the candy.

But when he stepped into the street, a ferocious ache surged through his stomach. It felt like a storm was brewing inside him.

He doubled over in pain.

"Fisher, watch out!" Ava screamed.

He glanced up just in time to see car headlights racing right toward him at full speed.

He put up his hands to block the blinding light, but before he had time to get out of the way . . .

The car plowed right into him.

21

ONLY THE DEAD CAN SPEAK TO THE DEAD

The minivan sped down the street. The rubber tires squealed as it disappeared around the corner.

"Fisher?" Ava cried out.

He was so stunned, he couldn't speak.

"Fisher, where are you?" he heard her say while she crawled around in the street, as if she were looking for lost keys.

"I'm right here," he said, but she didn't hear him.

Confused, he looked down at his hands. They were pale and translucent.

It worked! he thought, slightly horrified. *I'm a real ghost!*

He glanced in the direction where the mini-van had disappeared, realizing it had passed right through him.

"Ava, you need to eat three Monsterbars and then fly to the storm siren! It will paralyze the monsters until I can reverse the curse," he urged her.

But she couldn't hear him.

Knowing there wasn't much time, he stood and ran toward the nearby woods.

He hoped Ava would be okay without him. When he glanced over his shoulder, he saw her holding her broom and examining a candy wrapper in the moonlight.

Soon, his feet lifted off the ground, and he was hovering over a pile of leaves.

I'm—I'm flying! he thought in astonished wonder. *And on Halloween night!*

He soared over trees, houses, and lampposts. He swooped down and picked up an uneaten jack-o'-lantern from a darkened porch. He had never felt so free in all his life. Only now . . . he was dead.

A few moments later, Fisher landed outside the graveyard gates. An owl hooted nearby. Then another. As if in warning.

Fisher held the jack-o'-lantern in his spectral palms. Its perpetual candlelight glowed softly against the gray, slumbering fog. Dozens of spirits stood at the fence line of the cemetery, looking out into the woods, as if waiting for visitors.

It was the creepiest thing Fisher had ever seen.

But he no longer felt the chill of fear at the sight of the graves. He had *become* his fear—death—and it no longer held power over him.

He floated over the grass, navigating through the labyrinth of tombstones, until he arrived at the three side-by-side graves that bore his mother's maiden name.

Remembering the diary's prescription for conjuring the Dead, he set the jack-o'-lantern upon the middle grave and waited.

But nothing happened.

The night was dark and still, like the calm before a storm.

Soon, the moon peeked out from behind the gray clouds, and a thin path of moonlight dripped down from the sky and kissed the grave.

The flame inside the hollow pumpkin danced wildly. The jack-o'-lantern's face began to change. And a tall, ghoulish spirit rose up out of the candle and loomed above Fisher.

"Who dares wake me from my sleep?"

22

UNBURYING THE TRUTH

The ghost of Fisher's grandfather stared down at him. Fisher thought it strange that he still looked the same age he had in the newspaper photograph from thirty years before. The only difference was his pale, translucent appearance. That, and he was hovering a foot off the ground.

"I'm—I'm your grandson," Fisher introduced himself. "Hallie's my mom."

There was a long moment of silence. The specter seemed stunned, like he was processing what Fisher had said.

Fisher could see ethereal tears forming in his eyes.

"Welcome, boy," the man's ghost greeted him. "But—where is your grave? We weren't notified by the Council of your arrival."

He perused the cemetery for Fisher's freshly covered grave.

"I'm not really dead," Fisher tried to explain. "It's just temporary. At least I hope it is."

His grandfather's ghost squinted.

"Then how—and why—are you here?"

Fisher thought of the words written on the black candy wrapper. There was so much more that he wanted to ask his grandfather. But he knew he didn't have much time.

"It's my mom," he said. "She hates Halloween, and—"

"Hallie? Hates Halloween?" his grandfather questioned.

"Yeah, she thinks if she hadn't stayed out late trick-or-treating on Halloween night, you guys never would have gone looking for her. And you wouldn't have been killed in the accident."

"Looking for her?" he asked.

"Yeah," Fisher said. "The newspaper said that 'It is suspected that . . .'"

Fisher pulled out the obituary and pointed to the paragraph. His grandfather leaned over to read it.

After a moment, his grandfather looked up at him. Haunted by something.

"This obituary is . . . wrong," he said.

"What?" Fisher questioned.

"We knew where Hallie was all along," his grandfather revealed. "It was Halloween night, and we didn't want to rob her of an extra hour or two of making memories with her friends."

Fisher gulped. He suddenly felt colder.

"You mean—you weren't driving around town looking for her that night?"

"No. We went to Old Joe's Pumpkin Farm to do the corn maze one last time before they took it down. Our car slid on some smashed pumpkins in the road—that's what caused the accident."

Fisher was silent. Everything his mom had

been led to believe wasn't true.

"So it wasn't my mom's fault?" he asked.

His grandfather shook his head. "Far from it."

"I have to tell her somehow. I have to let her know the truth. It will change everything," Fisher said.

His grandfather put his fingers to his chin and brooded for a moment. Soon, his wraithlike eyes turned to his gravestone and his brows rose with an idea.

"There is one way I might be able to communicate to her," he said.

Fisher's grandfather held up his bony fingers and conjured a piece of paper out of thin air. Before he said anything, he held it up into the moonlight and used his glowing finger like a pen to write something secret upon it.

"Take this to her," he said. "If she sees this, she might understand."

Fisher took the paper and examined it. To him, it looked completely blank.

"Do you want to come with me?" Fisher asked. "To tell her yourself?"

His grandfather shook his head.

"Alas, even though tonight's the only night of the year we can be conjured from our eternal sleep, we spirits are bound to our graves. But tell your mom that we love her dearly," the phantom said.

"I will," Fisher promised.

He hugged his grandfather's ghost, wishing he had more time with him. He suspected it would be another seventy years or so before he would see him again.

Suddenly, a sour scent filled the air.

The candle in the jack-o'-lantern snuffed out.

And Fisher's grandfather disappeared.

Then Fisher heard . . .

Grrraaaagggghhhh!

Hisssss!

Aaahhhaaahhhaaa!

The monsters had found him.

23

HALLIE IS FOR HALLOWEEN

Out of the shadows, three monstrous silhouettes appeared. Fisher watched in horror as the vegetarian vampire sunk his fangs into the jack-o-lantern sitting atop the grave. All three monsters closed in around him. He then realized that, although living humans couldn't see his ghost form, the monsters still could.

He could smell their deathly stench as they reached toward him with handfuls of Monster-bars, eager to shove them into his mouth and make him fully one of them.

Fisher tried to jump in the air to fly away, but the vegetarian vampire grabbed his ankle and pulled him back down to the earth.

"Becooome onnne ooof ussss," the vampire moaned, gripping Fisher's throat and forcing open the ghost boy's jaws. The invisible candysnatcher stood beside him, shoving Monsterbars into Fisher's mouth, one by one.

"Eeeeaaat," Champ's monster-fied voice commanded.

The swamp creature squealed with delight, leaping around like a giant, possessed lizard.

Fisher tried to spit out the bars, but the monsters kept shoving more into his mouth. He tried again to escape, but the vampire bit his translucent arm just as the swamp creature projected slime all over him. Although Fisher was still in ghost form, the slime burned like alcohol being poured onto an open wound.

There's no escape now, he thought. *I'm doomed.*

Just then, a terrible sound blared throughout

the graveyard, vexing their eardrums. It sounded like a police siren being set off right next to them.

Only it wasn't the police.

It was . . .

Ava! Fisher realized. *She must have eaten the bars and used her broom to fly to the top of Town Hall and turn on the storm siren!*

Overwhelmed by the sound, the monsters let go of him and covered their ears. They fell to the ground beside him in torment.

Fisher spat out the Monsterbars and smiled, realizing that Ava had saved him and possibly the entire town.

"Sorry, guys," Fisher said to the monsters. "Gotta fly!"

Fisher's feet lifted off the ground once again. The monsters hissed and clawed at him as he floated over the iron gates, back toward town. He glanced over his shoulder and saw what looked like two tiny ghouls and a pair of painted blue legs stumbling out of the graveyard.

I have to hurry, he thought. *Before someone turns off the siren.*

The wind washed over Fisher like a strange, wondrous dream. From his view in the clouds, the houses in the neighborhood below looked like dollhouses stacked up next to each other.

Soon, the storm siren stopped, just as he had feared it would. Fisher assumed a city official had turned it off, but he hoped Ava's courageous act had bought him enough time to complete his mission.

Once he arrived at the end of Maple Street, he saw candlelight flickering in his upstairs bedroom window. He flew down to the house and floated through the wall.

His mom was sitting on the edge of his bed with her face buried in her hands, crying. He had never seen her like that. The pile of moving boxes sat in the corner, already filled with some of Fisher's stuff. In front of her was the photograph of her family dressed up for Halloween—the photo Fisher had left behind in the attic.

My mom must have gone up into the attic looking for me and found it, he thought.

As soon as Fisher landed beside her, a ghostly chill filled the room.

She looked up, as if sensing his presence.

Right then, the candle on his nightstand snuffed out. Fisher could hear his mom breathing in the dark. A moment later, the candle on the nightstand flickered back to life—this time, the flame was purple. The room danced with eerie shadows.

Fisher reached into his pocket and pulled out the crinkled sheet of paper his grandfather's ghost had given to him. It appeared to his mom that the paper was floating through the air on its own.

Her eyes were wide with wonder, horror, and confusion as it landed on top of the photograph.

Cautiously, she unfolded the paper and examined it.

Moonlight poured through the window and illuminated the back of the paper where Fisher's grandfather had inscribed something with his finger. To his mom's astonishment, a ghostly message materialized upon it:

> *It wasn't your fault, honey.*
> *We knew where you were the whole time.*
> *Sometimes, accidents just happen.*
> *It's time to let go.*
> *Love,*
> *Dad*
>
> *PS Always remember . . .*
> *Hallie is for Halloween.*

She stared at the paper for a long moment, her hands trembling as she examined her father's handwriting, which she hadn't seen in thirty years. She searched for breath but found none. As tears dropped from her eyes, she hugged the paper to her chest as if it were a long-lost treasure.

Fisher glanced out the window and saw the sky beginning to lighten. The sun was only a moment away from peeking over the horizon.

Just then, Fisher heard the front door down-stairs burst open.

And footsteps running up the stairs.

The monsters . . . he thought. *They're inside the house!*

24

TRANSFIGURATION

The monsters stomped up the stairs and pounded on the door to Fisher's bedroom.

"Run, Mom! Hurry!" he shouted, but she couldn't hear him.

He opened the window for her to escape, but she didn't move. Her eyes were closed, as if she was lost in a trance. She didn't seem the least bit fazed by the imminent attack of the monsters.

Knock! Knock! Knock!

The harder the monsters pummeled the door, the more the hinges began to creak.

Fisher knew there wasn't much time.

He hovered in front of his mom to protect her, but he knew he was practically powerless in his ghost form.

Just then, his mom's chest began to glow, softly, like a sun being born. A kaleidoscope of light spread out from her heart and into her veins, spider-webbing throughout her entire body. She looked otherworldly.

Then the magical light beamed out from her eyes, fingertips, and toes, scattering in all directions.

The bewitched luminescence shot through the bedroom door and into the hearts of each monster standing on the other side. It injected into Fisher's chest too, sending a rush of warmth over him. Lastly, the light zapped out the bedroom window and into the neighborhood, spreading to every pocket of town.

A monstrous miracle! Fisher thought as his pale existence began to materialize back into flesh and blood once again.

Suddenly . . .

He could feel his arms and legs.

He could taste and smell the pumpkin-scented air.

He touched his chest and could feel his heart beating.

He was alive!

His mom opened her eyes and grinned at the sight of him.

"Oh, Fisher!" she cried. "I'm so glad you're all right!"

She hugged him tightly, and he wrapped his arms around her. She felt soft against his skin.

"I'm so sorry, Mom. About your family. I—I didn't know," he said.

"It's okay," she replied. "Everything's okay now. I'm sorry I didn't listen to you, son."

He felt her warm tears dripping onto his forehead as they stood holding each other.

Then there was a loud knock on the door.

The monsters are still out there! Fisher thought, tensing in fright.

A familiar voice spoke. . . .

"Fisher? Is that you in there?"

It was Champ . . . the *real* Champ.

Fisher hurried to the door and opened it. There before him stood the Halloweeners, wearing their homemade costumes, looking just as they had the afternoon before.

"Guys!" Fisher shouted, tackling them with a hug.

"Where are we?" Pez asked, taking off his swamp creature mask and staring around in confusion.

Fisher smiled. "It's a long story."

Champ stuck his head out of the shirt of his tuxedo. "All I know is I'm huuunnngggrrry."

"Seriously?" Fisher questioned. "You just ate all the candy in town."

"Huh?" Champ replied, confused.

"Mmmm. Candy sounds good," Squirrel interjected. "I feel like I've been on one of my Mom's all-vegetable diets for weeks."

"And I feel like I just ran a hundred miles," Pez added. "Can I have some water?"

Fisher examined their faces but saw no sign that they were joking.

"You mean you guys really don't remember anything?"

Champ, Pez, and Squirrel looked at each other and shook their heads.

"The last thing I remember is going to the witch's house and seeing the candy cauldron. And then everything is black after that," Squirrel said.

"Yeah, and for some reason the 'Monster Mash' is stuck in my head," Champ added.

Fisher smirked knowingly.

"Guys, this is my mom. Mom, these are the guys I was telling you about," he said.

They all waved to her, and she waved back, still stunned by everything.

Pez scratched his chin, deep in thought. "You know, I do remember seeing Ava Highwater tricking Mrs. Sanderson, and—"

"Ava!" Fisher shouted.

He hurried past his mom, who sat down on the edge of his bed to look at her father's message again. He went straight to his telescope and peered through it into the neighborhood.

"That's not possible," Fisher whispered as the Halloweeners gathered around him.

The neighborhood looked spotlessly clean, as if the chaos of the night before had all been a dream. Town Square looked immaculate too. And the high school. And Food Mart. And even the drive-in.

For a moment, Fisher questioned if any of it had actually happened. He was afraid the Halloweeners might never believe him.

But then he saw Ava.

She was walking down the sidewalk holding her broom. She looked dazed, as if she couldn't quite remember what had happened either. Fisher smiled, glad to know she was safe.

He moved his telescope in the other direction to the far edge of the neighborhood, where Hidden Oaks Street dead-ended into the forest.

The dilapidated mansion looked like a sleeping beast, guarding its secrets.

Just then, the sun peeked over the horizon, and a golden beam of sunlight kissed the porch.

And right before Fisher's eyes, the cast-iron candy cauldron began to fade into a ghostly mist, until all at once it vanished.

Fisher felt someone's hand touch his shoulder.

"Halloween magic," his mom whispered in his ear.

25

HALLOWEEN FOREVER

The next day, the Halloweeners held a special meeting in their tree house. Fisher, Champ, Squirrel, and Pez sat around the tree-stump table, eating pizza and looking over the town gazette.

The headline read:

Midnight Mayhem:
Monsters Take Over Maple Street

A collage of photos was printed along with the article detailing the extraordinary events of Halloween night. There was a photo of the swamp creature climbing on the water tower, another of the vegetarian vampire silhouetted in front of the drive-in movie screen, and even one of the invisible candysnatcher dancing in the high school gym with his borrowed cane, cape, and top hat.

"I can't believe we did all of this—and all in one night," Pez said, observing another photo of his monster-fied self lapping water from a fire hydrant like a dog.

"Yeah, thank goodness no one knows it was us," Squirrel added as he gazed at a picture of himself devouring a pumpkin at Old Joe's Pumpkin Farm. "My parents would kill me if they knew we were the ones who sabotaged the festival."

"You saved us, Fish. You saved the whole town," Champ said.

"I'm just glad my mom said we don't have to move again. She's taking a full-time job at the high school," Fisher said.

"Heck yeah!" Champ cheered. "Now we can

camp out in the tree house every Friday night for the rest of the year!"

Fisher glanced at Pez, noticing he was deep in thought.

"You all right, Pez?"

Pez nodded.

"I've just been thinking—we all have monsters inside us that we have to face, right? Maybe sometimes it takes the help of friends to overcome them," Pez said.

"What are you talking about?" Champ asked, suspicious of Pez's mature persona.

"Well, even though I don't remember anything, I still feel different after what we went through. I woke up this morning and wasn't afraid of the water anymore. I even told my dad I'm going to try out for the swim team."

"I think I know what you mean," Champ affirmed. "For some unexplainable reason, I told my family that I'm going on their hike with them on Saturday. And they actually seemed like they were glad that I was going to come. It was like I wasn't invisible to them, even if just for once."

They all looked to Squirrel to see if he had anything meaningful to add.

"I . . ." Squirrel searched for something interesting to confess. "I ate a hamburger yesterday. And I didn't make my bed this morning."

The guys stared at him in disbelief. Champ laughed and patted Squirrel's shoulder.

"Oh, you're a wild man now, Squirrel," Champ teased. "Next thing you know, you'll be eating beef jerky and meatball sandwiches and not even tucking in your shirt!"

Sunlight filled the tree house as the boys' laughter echoed out over the graveyard.

Then the Halloweeners looked at each other and smiled at Fisher.

"You ready to take the oath?" Pez asked.

Fisher's eyes widened. It was the moment he had been waiting for. The moment he'd thought would never come.

"I'm ready," Fisher said. "But under one condition."

"What's that?" Pez asked.

"I'll become a Halloweener only if Ava can become one too," Fisher said.

There was a long moment of silence.

"Ava?" Squirrel asked incredulously. "As in . . . Ava Highwater?"

Fisher nodded. "Without her, we'd probably all be dead right now."

They all squinted, as if trying to process what Fisher was saying.

"You are talking about the leader of the Pumpkinheads?" Champ asked.

"Yeah. Only she's not a Pumpkinhead anymore. She belongs with us."

Champ, Squirrel, and Pez looked at each other. They knew they owed Fisher big-time, and if he was making a special request to let Ava join the club, well . . .

"All right, we'll let her in," Pez said, and the others reluctantly grunted in agreement. "But only if she'll help us win the Halloween Games next year."

"I promise you guys won't regret this," Fisher said excitedly.

"We already do," Champ assured him dryly, then smirked.

At their invitation, Fisher held up his right hand and put his left hand on the Halloweener Diary, then took the sacred oath every Halloweener in the history of Halloweeners had taken before him. It was so secret that he was told never to write it down or tell a soul.

Pez, Squirrel, and Champ then taught him the secret handshake . . .

And the ancient password . . .

And they even held his arm up like a champion boxer and declared him "Fisher—the Halloween King!"

Fisher was an official Halloweener.

For the first time, he noticed the faded photographs of past Halloweeners hanging on the western wall of the tree house. He smiled when he saw the one of his mom and several other kids sitting in that very same tree house thirty years before.

Beneath it were written the words:

Best Friends Forever

Fisher looked around at Champ, Pez, and Squirrel. He realized in that moment that someday, he might feel the same way about them too.

Right then, there was a knock on the floor door. The guys looked around at each other questioningly.

Fisher opened the door, and Ava appeared.

"Hi, guys," Ava said. "Thanks for the invitation, Fisher."

Champ's jaw dropped, and he and the others looked to Fisher for an explanation. "You invited her here before we agreed to let her join the club?"

"I knew you guys would make the right decision," Fisher said with a smirk.

Champ sighed, and the boys made Ava swear the oath right there on the spot. Then Champ put his hand out over the Halloweener emblem at the center of the tree-stump table.

Squirrel slapped his hand on top of Champ's.

Pez put his on top of Squirrel's.

Fisher on top of Pez's.

And Ava on top of Fisher's.

Then together, they spoke their sacred motto aloud: "Once a Halloweener . . . always a Halloweener. . . . Till death and beyond!"

ACKNOWLEDGMENTS

"I am a part of all that I have met."
—Alfred, Lord Tennyson

There are quite a few people to acknowledge here in this book of the Monsterstreet series:

First of all, my Mom, Dad, Sis—everything I am is because of you, and words can never express the depth of my gratefulness. I can only hope to honor you with the life I live and the works I create.

All my family: Granddad, Grandmom, Pappa Hugg, Mamma Hugg, Lilla, Meemaw, Nanny, GG, Grandmother Hugghins, Marilyn, Steve, Haddie, Jude, Beckett, Uncle Hal, Aunt Cathy, Nicole, Dylan, Aunt Rhonda, Uncle Greg,

Sam, Jake, Trey, Uncle Johnny, Aunt Glynis, Jerod, Chad, Aunt Jodie, Uncle Terry, Natalie, Mitchell, Anna, David, Hannah, David Nevin, Joy, Lukas, Teresa, and Aunt Jan.

Teachers, coaches, mentors, colleagues, and students: Jeanie Johnson, David Vardeman, Pat Vaughn, Lee Carter, Robert Darden, Kevin Reynolds, Ray Bradbury, R.L. Stine, Rikki Coke (Wiethorn), Peggy Jezek, Kathi Couch, Jill Osborne Wilkinson, Marla Jaynes, Karen Deaconson, Su Milam, Karen Copeland, Corrie Dixon, Nancy Evans Hutto, Pam Dominik, Jean Garner, Randy Crawford, Pat Zachry, Eddie Sherman, Scott Copeland, Heidi Kunkel, Brian Boyd, Sherry Rogers, Lisa Osborne, Wes Evans, Betsy Barry, Karen Hix, Sherron Boyd, Mrs. Kahn, Mrs. Turk, Mrs. Schroeder, Mrs. Battle, Mrs. McCracken, Nancy Frame Chiles, Mrs. Adkins, Kim Pearson, Mrs. Harvey, Elaine Spence, Barbara Fulmer, Julie Schrotel, Barbara Belk, Mrs. Reynolds, Vanessa Diffenbaugh, Elisabeth McKetta, Bryan Delaney, Talaya Delaney, Wendy Allman, John Belew,

Vicki Klaras, Gery Greer and Bob Ruddick, Greg Garrett, Chris Seay, Sealy and Matt Yates, David Crowder, Cecile Goyette, Kirby Kim, Mike Simpson, Quinlan Lee, Clay Butler, Mary Darden, Derek Smith, Brian Elliot, Rachel Moore, Naymond Keathley, Steve Sadler, Jimmy and Janet Dorrell, Glenn Blalock, Katie Cook, SJ Murray, Greg Chan, Lorri Shackelford, Tim Fleischer, Byron Weathersbee, Chuck Walker, John Durham, Ron Durham, Bob Johns, Kyle Lake, Kevin Roe, Barby Williams, Nancy Parrish, Joani Livingston, Madeleine Barnett, Diane McDaniel, Beth Hair, Laura Cubos, Sarah Holland, Christe Hancock, Cheryl Cooper, Jeni Smith, Traci Marlin, Jeremy Ferrerro, Maurice and Gloria Walker, Charlotte McDonald, Dana Gietzen, Leighanne Parrish, Heather Helton, Corrie Cubos, all the librarians, teachers, secretaries, students, custodians, and principals at Midway ISD, Waco ISD, Riesel ISD, and Connally ISD, all my apprentices at Moonsung Writing Camp and Camp Imagination, and to my hometown community of Woodway, Texas.

Friends and collaborators: Nathan "Waylon" Jennings, Craig Cunningham, Blake Graham, Susannah Lipsey, Hallie Day, Ali Rodman Wallace, Jered Wilkerson, Brian McDaniel, Meghan Stanley Lynd, Suzanne Hoag Steece, the Jennings family, the Rodman family, the Carter family, all the families of the "Red River Gang," the Cackleberries, the Geib family, Neva Walker and family, Rinky and Hugh Sanders, Clay Rodman, Steven Fischer, Dustin Boyd, Jeff Vander Woude, Randy Stephens, Allen Ferguson, Scott Lynd, Josh Zachry, Scott Crawford, Jourdan Gibson Stewart, Crystal Carter, Kristi Kangas Miller, Taylor Christian, Deanna Dyer Williams, Matt Jennings, Laurie McCool Henderson, Trey Witcher, Genny Pattillo Davis, Brady Williams, Brook Williams Henry, Michael Henry, Jamie Jennings, Jordan Jones, Adrianna Bell Walker, Sarah Rogers Combs, Kayleigh Cunningham, Rich and Megan Roush, Adam Chop, Kimberly Garth Batson, Luke Stanton, Kevin Brown, Britt

Knighton, George Cowden, Jenny and Ryan Jamison, Julie Hamilton, Kyle and Emily Knighton, Ray Small, Jeremy Combs, Mike Trozzo, Allan Marshall, Coleman Hampton, Kent Rabalais, Laura Aldridge, Mikel Hatfield Porter, Edith Reitmeier, Ben Geib, Ashley Vandiver Dalton, Tamarah Johnson, Amanda Hutchison Thompson, Morgan McKenzie Williams, Robbie Phillips, Shane Wilson, J.R. Fleming, Andy Dollerson, Terry Anderson, Mary Anzalone, Chris Ermoian, Chris Erlanson, Greg Peters, Doreen Ravenscroft, Brooke Larue Miceli, Emily Spradling Freeman, Brittany Braden Rowan, Kim Evans Young, Kellis Gilleland Webb, Lindsay Crawford, April Carroll Mureen, Rebekah Croft Georges, Amanda Finnell Brown, Kristen Rash Di Campli, Clint Sherman, Big Shane Smith, Little Shane Smith, Allen Childs, Brandon Hodges, Justin Martin, Eric Lovett, Cody Fredenberg, Tierre Simmons, Bear King, Brady Lillard, Charlie Collier, Aaron Hattier, Keith Jordan,

Greg Weghorst, Seth Payne, BJ Carr, Andria
Mullins Scarbrough, Lindsey Kelley Palumbo,
Cayce Connell Bellinger, David Maness,
Ryan Smith, Marc Uptmore, Kelly Maddux
McCarver, Robyn Klatt Areheart, Emily Hoyt
Crew, Matt Etter, Logan Walter, Jessica Talley,
JT Carpenter, Ryan Michaelis, Audrey Malone
Andrews, Amy Achor Blankson, Chad Conine,
Hart Robinson, Wade Washmon, Clay Gibson,
Barrett Hall, Chad Lemons, Les Strech,
Marcus Dracos, Tyler Ellis, Taylor Rudd, James
Yarborough, Scott Robison, Bert Vandiver,
Clark Richardson, Luke Blount, Allan Gipe,
Daniel Fahlenkamp, Ben Hogan, Chris Porter,
Reid Johnson, Ryan Stanton, Brian Reis, Ty
Sprague, Eric Ellis, Jeremy Gann, Jeff Sadler,
Ryan Pryor, Jared Ray, Dustin Dickerson, Reed
Collins, Ben Marx, Sammy Rajaratnam, Art
Wellborn, Cory Ferguson, Jonathan King, Jim
King, Anthony Edwards, Craig Nash, Dillon
Meek, Jonathan Stringer, the Bode and Moore
families, Jackie and Denver Mills, the Warrior

Poets, the Wild Hearts, the Barbaric Yawps, the Bangarang Brothers, and all the Sacred Circle guys (CARPE DIEM).

To all the writers, directors, composers, producers, artists, creators, inventors, poets, and thinkers who have shaped my life, work, and imagination—a list of luminaries which is far too long to mention here.

To Chris Fenoglio, for creating such stunning covers for the Monsterstreet series. It's safe to say your illustrations pass the ultimate test: they would have made me want to pick up the books when I was a boy! Thank you for lending your incredible talent and imagination to this project.

To the Stimola Literary Studio Family: Erica Rand Silverman, Adriana Stimola, Peter Ryan, Allison Remcheck, and all my fellow authors who are lucky enough to call the Stimola Literary Studio their home.

To the entire HarperCollins publishing family and Katherine Tegen family: Katherine

Tegen, David Curtis, Erin Fitzsimmons, Jon Howard, Robby Imfeld, Haley George, and Tanu Srivastava.

To my amazing agent, Rosemary Stimola, who plucked me out of obscurity, remained faithful to this project over the course of not just months but years, and who sets the highest standard of integrity within the wondrous world of children's publishing. I can't tell you how deeply grateful I am for all that you have done for me.

And to my extraordinary editor, Ben Rosenthal. From our very first conversation reminiscing about 1980s movies, I felt in my gut that you were a kindred spirit. Our collaboration on the Monsterstreet series has been one of the greatest joys and adventures of my life, and it's an enormous honor to get to share this journey with you. Thank you for all your guidance, encouragement, and optimism along the way . . . you've been a fantastic captain of this ship!

To my wife and best friend, Rebekah . . .

no words can ever tell you how grateful I am for the thousands of hours you've spent reading rough drafts, listening to unpolished ideas, and offering warm, thoughtful encouragement every step of the way. These books wouldn't exist without you, and I'm so glad I get to share this journey and all others by your side.

And lastly, to my most cherished treasures, my precious daughters, Lily Belle and Poet Eve: it is the greatest joy of my life to watch you gaze upon the world with wonder and tell us what you see. May stories always enchant you, and may you tell your own stories someday.

KEEP READING FOR A SNEAK PEEK AT ANOTHER
CHILLING MONSTERSTREET ADVENTURE

1

A STRANGE WIND

The two brothers stepped off the train, dragging their suitcases behind them. Ren was twelve, had perfectly combed hair, and wore his shirttail tucked in. Kip was nine, hadn't combed his hair in days, and wouldn't tuck in his shirt if his life depended on it.

It was their first time away from their parents for more than one night, and they had been given strict instructions to wait at the outdoor depot once they arrived at their destination. But when they looked around for somewhere to sit down, they realized that they were the only ones there.

"This place gives me the creeps," Ren said.

"Scaredy-cat," Kip replied. "What time is Aunt Winnie supposed to pick us up?"

"Four o'clock sharp," Ren said, glancing down at his watch.

A crow cawed, and the boys turned to see a murder of black birds flying away from a scarecrow in the nearby cornfield. The brittle shucks quivered as a cool October breeze swept over Ren and Kip, carrying a strange scent upon it.

"Do you smell that?" Ren asked.

"Yeah. Smells like . . . pumpkins," Kip said. "And cotton candy."

"And something else too. What is it?" Ren mused aloud.

"I don't know, but can you help me carry this?" Kip asked, tugging at his suitcase, which was twice his size.

"You're old enough to carry your own luggage," Ren said, forgetting about the scent for a moment.

"But it's too heavy," Kip complained. "And mom said you're supposed to look after me while we're here."

"Only because she doesn't want you to get in trouble like you always do," Ren said, then reluctantly helped Kip pull his suitcase to a nearby bench. "I swear, Mom and Dad should pay me for being your full-time babysitter."

"They don't pay you because brothers are *supposed* to look out for each other," Kip said. "Clay Ferguson's big brother takes him on bike rides and to get ice cream and even to the movies. They're like . . . friends."

"Well, if you weren't so annoying, maybe I'd let you tag along too," Ren replied. "Not all of us can do whatever we want when we want— there's a little thing called responsibility."

"Hey, I can be responsible," Kip said.

"Yeah right. When was the last time you made your bed or helped Mom unload the dishwasher?"

Kip didn't say anything.

"It's the same everywhere we go," Ren said. "I have to be the responsible one while you get to have all the fun."

Kip looked at the ground, and Ren could tell he had hurt his little brother's feelings.

Just as he was about to apologize, a black hearse with tinted windows slowly rolled into the empty parking lot and stopped. Chills shot up Ren's spine as he realized that whoever was inside it was staring right at them.

2

LAND OF THE DEAD

The hearse didn't move. It just sat there with the engine still running, like a spider waiting patiently in the shadows of its web.

"Should I call the cops?" Ren whispered, but Kip looked more curious than afraid.

Ren felt his breath quickening as he peered at the dark windshield glaring back at them.

What do they want? he wondered.

Suddenly, the engine turned off.

The driver door creaked open.

And a pair of black tennis shoes appeared.

A brown-haired woman wearing sunglasses

and a nurse's uniform stepped out of the hearse and waved at them. She looked a few years younger than their mom.

"Aunt Winnie?" Ren said in disbelief.

"Hi, boys!" she called. "Sorry, I had to take a moment to touch up my makeup."

They met her at the bottom of the depot steps, and she gave them both hugs.

"I swear you two have grown a foot since last Thanksgiving! I'm so glad I get you for an entire week while your parents are away on their anniversary trip in Europe. We're going to have so much fun!"

Ren had always liked Aunt Winnie more than his other aunts and uncles. She was the only older person he knew who really seemed to care about what a kid had to say. Plus, she always sent the best birthday presents.

"What's with the hearse?" Kip asked. "Do you work for a funeral home or something?"

Aunt Winnie laughed.

"Something like that," she teased. "Let's get your bags in the back with the coffin, and I'll take you to . . . the Land of the Dead!"

"The Land of the Dead?" Ren questioned.

But Aunt Winnie didn't explain.

As they drove through the nearby neighborhood, Ren observed Halloween décor in every yard. There were blow-up monsters and fake gravestones, smoking witch's cauldrons and light-up animatronic figures. It seemed every house in town went all out for Halloween.

All the while, the pumpkin-candy scent poured through the hearse's open windows.

"Don't you just love this time of year?" Aunt Winnie said. "I can't believe Halloween is only a few days away. Did you boys bring costumes? If not, I can throw something together for you."

"I think I'll pass," Ren said. "Every Halloween, I end up spending the entire night chasing after Kip and making sure he doesn't get in trouble."

"I can help watch Kip so that you can have fun too," Aunt Winnie replied.

"Really?" Ren asked.

"Sure," Aunt Winnie said. "I mean, we're

talking about Halloween here. The one night of the year you can become anything you want! Besides, you're only a kid once."

Ren half smiled. The idea of actually getting to have fun on Halloween sounded too good to be true.

A few minutes later, Aunt Winnie turned in to a long driveway, and Ren observed the rusted iron sign above the arched stone entrance. It was overgrown with twisting green vines, but he could still make out the words *Old Manor Nursing Home.*

"You work at a nursing home?" Ren asked.

"You boys will love it," Aunt Winnie said. "It's like living in a library, only the books can talk to you. I've wanted to work here since I was in college. So when they invited me to be their activities director, I jumped at the opportunity. There's something special about helping people during their last stop in life, you know."

"Creepy is more like it," Kip mumbled.

Ren elbowed Kip in his ribs.

"That sounds nice, Aunt Winnie," Ren said,

then glared at Kip and added, "and responsible."

Kip rolled his eyes.

Once inside the property grounds, Ren expected to see dozens of old people wandering around in the garden while others sat in wheelchairs staring out into nothingness. But instead, he saw pumpkins grinning from behind each window, black streamers strung above every door, and droves of elderly people cobwebbing the porch.

"Welcome to the Land of the Dead," Aunt Winnie announced.

Ren looked up and saw a giant hand-painted sign hanging over the front doors of the nursing home.

Beware . . .
You Are Now Entering the Haunted Manor!

"*This* is the Land of the Dead?" Kip asked. "Do you call it that because people die here all the time?"

"Kip!" Aunt Winnie said. "We're actually just transforming Old Manor into a big haunted house for Halloween night—the Haauuunntted Maaannnooooorrr!" she said in her spookiest voice. "I've put ads in the local gazette, inviting all the neighborhood kids to come trick-or-treating here. I even rented this hearse for the week to keep parked out front to give it extra ambience."

"You're not going to need to put much makeup on these old people for your haunted house," Kip said, then pointed to the small graveyard in the empty field next to the manor. "Everyone here already looks half-dead."

Ren nudged Kip again.

"Kip, please show a little respect while you're here," Aunt Winnie said. "These folks have lived stories beyond your wildest dreams. And as you can see, they're quite fond of Halloween. I spent half our annual activities budget at the Halloween store. Maybe you boys can help us finish decorating. There are still quite a few boxes to bring up from the basement, and I could use some help getting this coffin inside."

As the boys stepped out of the hearse, a crinkled sheet of paper twirled in the strange autumn wind and blew up against Ren's shin. He picked up the flyer and read it.

Experience the horror, the mystery, the wonder!

Get your ticket to the scariest carnival in the world.

But beware . . . you may not make it out alive.

*Bring this flyer to the Carnival of Horrors for one free ride!

Ren looked up and saw a giant black Ferris Wheel looming in the distance, reaching toward the gray October sky. The wheel was surrounded by a tiny village of orange-and-black-striped tents and rusty rides, all dotted with alluring purple lights. At the sight of it all, Ren realized what the peculiar scent had been.

The carnival! he thought. *With its funnel cakes and cotton candy, turkey legs and roasted corn, and a thousand other autumn delights* . . .

But there had been something else in the scent too—something he still couldn't name.

Aunt Winnie stepped out of the car and noticed the flyer in Ren's hand.

"You know, it's weird," she said. "I woke up this morning, and that Halloween carnival had just appeared overnight. No trains. No trucks. Nothing. It's like it conjured itself out of thin air."